# Confessions of a Dope Boy

### First Lady K

D1557211

UF
First La

## Preface

*Beep. Beep. Beep.* Quinton woke up slowly to the sound of the machines beeping. Everything was blurry as he tried to focus on where he was. *Where the hell am I?* He thought. All he saw was white walls and ceilings. The room smelled of bleach and disinfectant. He tried to lift himself up but everything on his body felt like bricks. *Yo what the fuck happened?* He questioned himself. He tried to open his mouth when he heard someone else in the room.

*"Quinton? Oh my God he's awake!"* the young girl rushed to his side. *"Quinton can you hear me? Don't try to talk. Oh my God. Thank you Jesus!"* she rambled off. She grabbed his hand and squeezed it. It was then he saw he was wearing a hospital bracelet with his name on it, Quinton White. He tried again to open his mouth but nothing came out.

*"Don't try to talk. I'm gonna go get the doctor."* she released his hand and ran out to get a doctor.

Quinton lay there attempting to sit up. He couldn't

understand why he was so groggy. Before he could move any further, a tall white male came into the room with a chart. Behind him followed a black nurse with what appeared to be a need in her hand.

*"Well hello Mr. White."* The doctor greeted him as he walked in. The nurse walked past and began to check his vitals while the doctor went over his chart.

*"You are a very lucky man Mr. White."* The doctor told him. *"Try not to speak. I know you have a thousand questions racing through your mind, but right now your jaw is wired shut until it can heal properly."* He informed him.

Quinton frowned at what he heard and became aware of the metal that he felt in his mouth. He was starting to really wake up and listen to the man in front of him. The nurse continued to check his vitals and changed his fluid bag. *Where the hell do I know her from?* he thought to himself. The more she moved around him, the more familiar she looked. She paid him no attention as she continued to do her job.

*"Mr. White, you've been here for about three weeks now. You were brought in with multiple shot wounds and lost a lot of blood. We were able to remove three of the bullets however; one is lodged into your shoulder blade, so we will try again to remove the bullet once we know you are more stable and that your body will be able to stand it. But, for right now, you're out of immediate danger. It's going to be difficult for you. I won't lie to you. You are very lucky to be alive."* He told Quinton.

Quinton continued to stare at him as the doctor rambled.

*"It's actually amazing."* The doctor continued. *"We had one gentleman die from a single bullet and here you are with four expected to make a full recovery."* He said.

Quinton frowned and rolled his eyes up. The nurse came forward with the needle and inserted the medicine in his tube.

*"What's that you're are giving him?"* the young girl asked. She had been exceptionally quiet throughout the time the doctor had been in the room.

*"It's just a sedative to help Mr. White relax and sleep."* The

nurse answered quietly as she finished the medicine.

Quinton started to frown up again. *I just fucking woke up.,* he thought to himself.

*"I don't understand. He just woke up. Why is he being put back to sleep so fast? Shouldn't you be trying to figure out who did this to him?"* she asked holding back tears.

The doctor reached over the cabinet and retrieved some tissues for the girl. *"I understand your questions."* He said as he handed her the tissues to wipe her face. *"But that is a matter for the police to handle, not a doctor. Our job is to save his life, not try to figure out who almost stole it."* He said.

The young girl began to cry again at the thought of Quinton being gone.

The doctor came over and held her hand as they watched Quinton drift to sleep.

*"It's going to be ok. He's been through a lot. Better that he rest now. Because he has a hell of a battle ahead."*

**Chapter One**

*"Look at your neighbor and say neighbor!"*

*"Neighbor"* the congregation followed suit.

*"Oh neighbor!"* he said.

*"Oh neighbor."*

*"I don't know about you but, it's my time!"* he screamed into the microphone.

Bishop White looked down from his pulpit at his congregation and he smiled. He knew he was doing what God ordained for him to do when he came to the church. He looked out at all the faces looking back at him and was proud. When he began ministering, it was a small congregation of about twenty people in a small gym, and now, he had over 10,000 members in one of the largest churches in Atlanta, Georgia. Pearly Gates Baptist Church was one of the most predominately Black churches and thanks to the members, he was the leading pastor.

He looked at the teleprompter to see a message letting him know that the ushers were preparing for the offering. He nodded to his son Quinton who was working the booth to acknowledge that he saw the message. He was bringing what he liked to call his "Holy Ghost Hype" up when he saw a younger girl walking down the aisle. He had seen her in the church on a consistent basis, and the two had exchanged a few looks. He was starting to get aroused just watching her walking. He shook his thoughts and tried to focus on his congregation. He glanced to his let and saw his wife Anna frowning at him. He tried not to pay it too much attention.

*It's not as if I'm actually doing anything*, he thought to himself. Men look just as much as women. *Just because I'm a Bishop don't mean I can't look. Shoot back in the day I would have had both of them no question.* Bishop knew he was wrong to be having lustful thoughts, but as long as he wasn't acting on them, he figured he was fine. But he already knew he was going to hear it from Anna later. He made a mental note to take her out somewhere to get her mind off it. He turned back to the pulpit and began to speak.

*"Brothers and sisters, it is now time to give back. Now we all*

*know that the Bible says that we as Christians are to tithe ten percent of what we earn. But church today, I challenge you to tithe twenty percent. Can we do that? Can you meet your Bishops challenge today?"* he asked.

The church applauded and the Bishop continued.

*"Now Saints, we are in for a treat today. Our very own Sister LaKeisha Wyatt is going to bless us with a song. Sister Wyatt."* He motioned to her to come forward and walked to his seat. LaKeisha walked to the microphone as the congregation applauded.

*<u>"The race is not given, to the swift, nor to the strong. But to the one that endureth, until the end. There will be problems. And sometimes, you walk alone. But I know that I know, that I know. Things will work out, yes they will. For the good, of them. For the good of them. Who loves the Lord."</u>*

The Bishop sat in his seat and closed his eyes. To the congregation, he looked to be into the song that LaKeisha was singing, but in reality, he was getting his thoughts together. He felt a change coming, but he wasn't sure what. He looked over at

LaKeisha who was now belting out the notes and several church members were standing up feeling the spirit. He began to listen to the words that she was singing.

*"Sometimes, you may have to cry. And sometimes, you may have to move! That I know, that I know, that I know, that I know, that I know, things will work out yes they will! For the good of them. For the good of them. Who loves, loves the Lord? I came to tell ya, you can't stop it. They will come, but don't, don't, don't you worry. I know that it will. Yaaaaaasssss it will yes!"*

Bishop nodded his head as he let the music move him. He looked over at his family sitting in the wing and thought about everything that he had been through, but couldn't shake his thoughts of how his life used to be. He looked at his wife Anna. He loved her so much. She was the definition of a true supporter and had been down with him since day one. She stood by him when he was out on the streets slanging and banging, trying to hustle. She dealt with all of his bull and the jealous females, pregnancy scares, and the secret child that he tried to hide from her. He looked over at his son Quinton and thought about how he wasn't really there for him in the early years because he was scared that Anna would've left him. Quinton was now 18, and he was proud. He looked at his daughter Traniece and smiled. Traniece was his proud and joy. When he found out Anna was pregnant with her he made sure he was there for her, for both his kids. She was now fifteen and he wanted to protect her from any and everything.

Bishop stood to his feet as the soloist finished and walked up to the pulpit.

*"Well church I don't know about ya'll but, that song moved me. Did it move you?"* he asked.

*"Yes!"* the congregation shouted.

*"It don't sound like you been blessed church. Now did it move you?"* he shouted.

*"Yes!"* the congregation yelled again with more enthusiasm.

*"All right now."* He said, *"That's what I need to hear. Family, take your Bibles out and turn to the book of Matthew Chapter 6 versus 5-15. I'm reading from the King James Version. If you don't*

*have a Bible share with your neighbor, or pull it up on your iPad or*

*iPhone or Android or tablet and when you found it, say amen."*

Bishop instructed.

*"Amen"* the congregation began to speak as people slowly

found the page containing the verse.

*"And it reads:*

*5 And when thou prayest, thou shalt not be as the hypocrites are:*

*for they love to pray standing in the synagogues and in the corners of*

*the streets, that they may be seen of men. Verily I say unto you, They*

*have their reward.  6 But thou, when thou prayest, enter into thy*

*closet, and when thou hast shut thy door, pray to thy Father which is*

*in secret; and thy Father which seeth in secret shall reward thee*

*openly.7 But when ye pray, use not vain repetitions, as the heathen*

*do: for they think that they shall be heard for their much speaking.8*

*Be not ye therefore like unto them: for your Father knoweth what*

*things ye have need of, before ye ask him.9 After this manner*

*therefore pray ye: Our Father which art in heaven, Hallowed be thy*

*name.10 Thy kingdom come, Thy will be done in earth, as it is in heaven.11 Give us this day our daily bread.12 And forgive us our debts,*

*as we forgive our debtors.13 And lead us not into temptation, but*

*deliver us from evil: For thine is the kingdom, and the power, and the*

*glory, forever. Amen.14 For if ye forgive men their trespasses, your*

*heavenly Father will also forgive you: 15 But if ye forgive not men*

*their trespasses, neither will your Father forgive your trespasses.*

Bishop closed his Bible and took his reading glasses off. *"Let*

*the word of God be a blessing to those willing to receive. You may be*

*seated."* He instructed. *"Church today, I want to talk to you about*

*letting go, and letting God....."*

*

Quinton was sitting in the pew trying to pay attention to his

father's sermon. He was tired because the night before he had gone

out to party with his boys and didn't get in until three in the

morning. His father thought he was sleep but really he was out

having fun.

*Hell what he don't know won't hurt him,* Quinton thought. He

knew that if his father found out anything that he was doing, he would have a cow and two chickens. It wasn't like his hands were completely dirty. He just liked having a little bit of fun. So what if he was skipping school? *The shit is boring anyway*, he thought. He snuck out at night because his father and step mother had him on some dumb ass curfew. *Eighteen years old and I got a damn curfew*, he thought to himself. *It don't make no damn sense.* Quinton didn't get what his father was always riding him about being this good boy. *Hell that nigga did some shady ass shit back in the day*, he thought to himself. *Clearly him and moms was banging and wasn't even married. Hell, moms was nothing but a side piece to him, so he can dead all that other shit.*

Quinton's mother told him about how she and Bishop met. Bishop was in the streets hard and she worked in one of his spots. She had started out being a look out for the crew but Bishop had a soft spot and a hard rock for pretty girls with big booties and wanted her up under him. She told her sister that initially that she tried to stay away from him because she knew he had a girl and she wasn't trying to be anybody's sideline piece. Plus Anna was the type of chic you didn't try. Everybody on the block knew Anna because she made it clear that Bishop was her man, from the blinged out piece she wore, to the chromed out Mercedes Benz with the license plate that read BISHOPS1. Anna was not the one to mess with. She always made sure that when she stepped out, she was amazing from the root of her hair to the tip of her toes. And Bishop was proud to have her on his arm. He just couldn't stay away from the women. Even after Anna beat down the last chic, and damn near tore all his stuff up, he couldn't stay away. When he met, Tanya, Quinton's mother, he tried to resist but when he saw her, he knew he had to have her.

It started off friendly with him offering her rides home from the house after her "shift" was over. At first, she declined but one night, her ex-boyfriend decided he wanted to pop up and try to act as if he had something to prove. He scared Tanya and she ran in the house with him following her and running up into a new world of trouble. Bishop and his boys beat him down and she never saw him again. Bishop gave Tanya a ride home that night and before she knew what was happening, they were both rolling around on her living room floor doing things no one could imagine. Tanya was sprung after that but she never took it there unless he initiated it. Their relationship carried on like that for six months with her working for him and getting extra benefits. It wasn't until she found out that she was pregnant that Bishop flipped. He stopped calling her and ignored her when she was putting in work for him. He put her back on look out and distanced himself from her. Tanya remembered the exact words he said to her.

*"I got a girl. I can't be no help if she know I got a baby. I'll do what I can but you can't be bringing the baby around or nothing like that."* Bishop told her.

She had tears in her eyes and despite her being upset and hurt, she did what he asked. She decided that she didn't need him to raise her baby, until after she had Quinton. When she looked into her beautiful baby boy's eyes, she knew that he didn't deserve the way that he was being treated. She tried calling and texting Bishop but he always ignored her.

One day when Quinton was about six months old, she got the courage to go to his house. Not many people knew where he lived but because he was sloppy when it came to the females, but Tanya as special to him so he took her there several times before. She waited until early in the morning when she knew that both of them would be home. She rang the bell and fidgeted waiting on the door to open. When it did, stood Anna in one of Bishops tee shirts with her hair in a disheveled ponytail atop her head.

*"Do you know what fucking time it is knocking on the damn door at six in the damn morning?!"* Anna spat out to the woman.

*"I—I—I'm sorry. I was trying to see if Bishop was home."* Tanya stammered.

Anna stood her stance at the door and if looks could kill, Quinton would be an orphan. *"What the fuck do you want with my nigga?"* Anna looked closer at her. *"Ain't you the chic that work in the warehouse?"* she asked.

Tanya stood there holding Quinton feeling lower than ever. *"Yea."* She answered. *"Look I don't want any trouble. I just--- I needed to talk to Bishop."* Quinton began to fuss and Anna acknowledged what Tanya was holding.

18

Anna's eyes grew large as she saw the bundle moving. *"I know you ain't tryna pin your baby on my man. Bitch you better be glad that baby is in your hands cause that's the only thing saving your life right now!"*

By this time, Anna was yelling and Bishop was coming down the stairs to see what the commotion was.

*"Babe what the hell are you screaming about? You tryna wake the neighbors?"* he said as he walked up to the door. All the color drained from his face when he saw Tanya standing there with Quinton in her arms. He hadn't seen her since before she had the baby so he didn't expect this.

Anna turned and tried to hit him but he blocked her before she could. Playing stupid he asked, *"What the hell is wrong with you Ann?"*

*"What the hell is wrong with me? How about this bitch showing up with a fucking baby that looks like you? That's what the hell is wrong with me!"* she said pointing towards Tanya.

*"Okay first of all you need to calm down. We don't need to be*

19

*out here screaming and making all this noise. I'm sure someone has probably called the cops by now and we can't afford to have them run up in my spot."* Bishop said pushing Anna inside and leaving the door open for Tanya. Tanya tiptoed into the house and stood at the hallway.

*"You bring this bitch in our house? Really Bishop? All because she shows up with a baby? So that means you fucked her! I'm so sick of this shit. Fuck you! I don't need this shit!"* Anna yelled as she stomped up the stairs slamming the door to their bedroom.

Bishop sighed and walked to the couch to sit down. Tanya did not move from where she was standing. Bishop knew Anna was upstairs probably tearing up everything that he owned.

*"What the fuck were you thinking coming here Tanya?"* he hissed at her.

Tanya was fighting back the tears. *"Look Bishop I really didn't want to. But, I can't raise him knowing that his father is capable of taking care of him, but won't because he's afraid to lose his woman. Quinton is your son Bishop. I didn't make him by myself.*

*How can you just go from telling me I was the most special thing in the world one day to denying your son the next?"* she asked. *"Look at him Bishop!"* she yelled at him as she held the baby up. *"You look at him and tell me that this is not your son."*

Bishop knew the minute he laid eyes on him that he was his son. He just didn't want to lose Anna. She was his world. But he knew he couldn't deny his son. He didn't deserve it. Bishop grew up without his father, which was one of the main reasons he was in the streets now. He didn't know how he was going to do it, but he had to be there for him.

*"Can I hold him? I mean is it ok?"* he asked.

Tanya hesitated before she handed him to him. Bishop looked down at him and he felt a lump in his throat. *"Damn. I'm sorry T. I fucked up. I got caught up and trying to keep everybody happy. I fucked up bad. It wasn't supposed to happen like this."* he said as a tear fell down his face looking into the eyes of his son. Bishop was so busy looking at the baby that he didn't see Anna around the corner.

*"You fucking bitch!"* she screamed as she jumped Tanya from behind and began punching her repeatedly. Tanya was caught off guard and tried to fight off as best as she could. She fought back throwing punches at Anna. Bishop put Quinton down and ran over to separate the two.

*"Yo! Anna chill! You can't be hitting here! She got a baby!"* he grabbed Anna and put her against the wall holding her tight so she couldn't get to Tanya again.

Tanya walked over to the baby picking him up and began to walk to the front door. *"I can't have our child around this. He doesn't deserve this. Just call me when you ready to see your son and not have all this drama around and maybe we'll be here."* She stormed out.

*"FUCK!"* Bishop yelled.

*"Yea fuck is right."* Anna said with tears streaming down her face. She broke free from him and walked to the bag she had sat by the door. *"Fuck her, and fuck you."* She cried out as she walked out the door.

*

"*Hallelujah!*" Quinton snapped out of his thoughts when he heard the congregation shouting. His father was getting into the heart of his sermon and almost the entire church was hollering. Quinton wanted to get up and walk out but knew he couldn't. That was unacceptable as a preacher's kid. They were always expected to act a certain way and be on their best behavior. A preachers kid was the last one that anyone wanted to hear gossip about. Quinton hated when everyone told him how they thought he should act. He wasn't the preacher, his father was. Why did he have to be punished for his father's lifestyle? *I'm my own person*, he thought. *I wish they would let me live my own life.* He looked up to see Anna frowning at him.

"*Pay attention.*" She mouthed.

Quinton rolled his eyes and sat pretending to pay attention to his father. He felt a buzz in his pocket that continued to go off. Quinton checked his phone to see who was texting him during church. Not that he was really paying attention anyway, but he wasn't trying to hear his father's mouth, and he was already pissed that he had been skipping school. He pulled his phone out and saw his boy Read had sent him a message about getting up later.

*Read: Wat up PK? You headed to the spot later?*

Quinton smirked when he read the text message. Reid had nicknamed him PK ever since he met him. He was fifteen and was walking to the store when a group of guys had jumped him trying to steal his sneakers. He could definitely hold his own and was fighting them off when he saw Read come out of nowhere and start throwing punches like he was Muhammad Ali. Quinton looked up to see who the stranger helping him was, stood up on his feet and squared up.

*"Aye my nigga you cool. Ain't no beef here. Just doing a good deed."* He said with a sarcastic laugh.

Quinton looked at him skeptically.

*"Good look."* He said.

*"No problem son."*, the young boy responded. *"Where you*

*from kid?"* he asked.

*"Right here in the A. The name is Quinton but they call me Q."* he answered brushing dirt off his clothes.

*"What up son? The block calls me Read. I read a nigga quick and can tell what they about"* He said proudly. The two dapped each other up.

*"Aye yo son you gotta be careful coming around these parts. Niggas be looking ready to jack a nigga for his paper."* Read told him. *"Where you headed to anyway?"* he asked.

Quinton looked around to make sure no surprises were coming. *"I gotta head over to my pops church."* He said.

Read looked him up and down and hid eyes grew large.

*"Yo I knew you looked familiar! Aye ain't your pops name Bishop?"* Read asked him.

Quinton contemplated telling him a lie but Read looked like he knew more than he was letting on, and he did help him from getting beat down, so he just shook his head yes.

*"Yea. That's my pops. He just became the pastor a few years ago."* Quinton told him.

Read stood in amazement. He ran with Bishop when he first moved to Atlanta from New York so he was in awe that he was meeting his son. Everyone respected Bishop in the streets. Before he turned his life over to God, Bishop was that nigga. He never had to check his crews because they knew not to cross him. Many tried to be like him but none of them could come near his stature. Bishop always was hungry for the paper and the power and kept his family fed. When Read first moved to Atlanta, Bishop hired him as his runner and before he knew it, he was one of the youngest members to work in Bishops trap. Read idolized Bishop and it bothered him when he decided to give his hustle up. He knew he had helped Quinton for something. He definitely had to look out for him because he felt like he owed Bishop for all the help he had given him.

*"Man, your pops was my dude. I used to work for him in the trap. Hell cause of him I'm one of the most paid men in the game. Your pops put me on fresh off the bus son. I appreciate that nigga*

*man real talk."* Read said seriously.

Quinton never really heard anyone talk about his father before he became a pastor. It was like he completely blacked out that part of his life. *"Word?"* he asked him.

*"Yea man. Yo man, your pops is like a legend in these streets son. Bishop gets mad respect."*

*"He don't ever really talk about it much."* Quinton told him. *"I knew my mom's told me he was a drug dealer a long time ago but, I thought he was just nickel and diming. I didn't know he was that major."*

Read laughed. *"Man please! Nickel and diming is what these little kindergartners are out here doing. Your pops is like kingpin. Yo son, your pops may be a Bishop now but he wasn't always about that life."*

Quinton was puzzled by everything that he was hearing. He didn't want to come off naïve but everything that Read was telling him he just couldn't believe. *"Wow."* Was all he could say.

*"Yea man. Real talk. Yo I'm headed to the trap in a little bit. You should come through so you can meet the crew."* He told him.

Quinton was hesitant but didn't let on. He knew his father would definitely disapprove of him hanging around someone in the streets but he wanted to know about his father before the Holy Bible. Quinton agreed to meet up with him later.

*"Aight man cool. Go on and head to the church house. Don't worry I'm gonna check these little ass niggas around here. You ain't gotta worry about that. Niggas on my shit anyway."* Read said.

The two dapped each other up again and Quinton headed to the church.

\*

Bible study had let out and Quinton decided to go see what Read was talked about. He walked up the sidewalk to the address of the trap house. He saw two guys sitting on the porch staring him down. *Damn I look like a fucking square*, he thought as he realized he was wearing slacks, a dress shirt and some sneakers. He had Bible study on Wednesdays at the church, and even though it was casual dress, his father preferred him and his sister to be dressy. As he got closer he tried to change his demeanor and become more nonchalant and tough. Internally, he was shaking and nervous inside because he didn't want to get jumped again. He got closer to the gate and he saw one of the boys reaching for his gun.

"*Wassup? What you lost or something church boy?*" the boy asked.

Quinton puffed out his chest and put some bass in his voice. "*Nah nothing like that. I'm here to see Read. He told me to come through.*" Quinton was hoping Read would come outside and see him so he could stop sweating.

"*Aye homie, ain't no Read here, so, you needs to keep it moving.*" The other boy said not leaving his post.

Quinton stood at the end of the walkway and contemplated walking up anyway. He knew they could shoot him from where they were so he decided against it. He turned to walk off when he heard the front door open.

"*Aye yo Q, what's good my nigga?!*" Read yelled.

29

Quinton turned around to see Read trotting down the steps to the house with the two boys watching.

*"Was good man?"* Quinton said calmly. *"Yea I was about to head out cause your bodyguards said you wasn't here."* He said sarcastically as he looked at them.

The two boys didn't flinch. *"We don't know you homey."* One spoke up. *"We gotta protect ours. For all we know, you the police. Hell Read how the fuck you don't know he the cops?"* he asked boldly.

Reads jaw clinched and Quinton sat and watched amused. *"First of all little nigga, don't ever fucking question me about who the fuck I bring around. Remember, I feed you nigga. Don't bite the hand that feeds you. If it wasn't for his pops, you niggas wouldn't be eating now."* He said pointing to Quinton.

The boy looked down at his feet and didn't say a word. The other boy who idly sat and watched quietly asked, *"Who's his pops?"*

Read smiled and said *"Bishop."*

You could see both boys thinking quickly to figure out who it was. The quiet one got excited. *"Bishop?! You mean like Bishop the king of the fucking A Bishop?! Oh shit! This shit is crazy! Ay yo man, your pops was the shit!"* he said excited.

The other boy who got checked just stood there watching as if he wasn't amazed. Quinton could tell he was embarrassed cause he got checked in front of him. He tried to play it cool cause he didn't want them to know that he didn't know much about his father's past.

*"Yea man. That's what I'm hearing."* He said coolly.

*"Aye man come on in the crib nigga. Let's get out this damn cold ass air."* Read began to walk up the steps to the door.

Quinton followed behind him and the younger boy was excited and telling him about the area. Quinton kept his eye on the older boy. Something told him he would be trouble later.

When he got inside, Quinton took a look around and saw several guys in the living room sitting down watching two guys play Madden on PS3. He passed by the kitchen area to see several stacks of weed and coke on the table and an older woman that was stirring a pot and appeared to be cooking. What she was cooking he didn't know, but he made sure not to look too long so as not to bring any unnecessary attention to himself. He followed Read to another room which he guessed was a bedroom that he turned into a second living room. Read sat down on the couch and Quinton took a seat in the chair across from it. The older boy that sized him up and down never followed so Quinton relaxed a little. The younger boy came in and leaned against the wall.

*"Wow man. I didn't know Bishop had a son."* He said. *"Aye how old you is man?"* he asked him.

*I can tell he doesn't go to school,* Quinton thought to himself. *"Fifteen."* He answered.

*"That's wassup. I'm fourteen. Aye I'm Lil G."* he introduced himself dapping him up.

The three sat in the room and talked about how bad Bishop was back in the day and how he was a living legend. Lil G told him about how he got forced into the game when his mother lost her job and couldn't afford to take care of him and his three younger sisters. As the oldest child in the house, he dropped out of school to start hustling full time to help his mom pay bills. She didn't like what he was doing, but she didn't turn the money away either. The older boy, who Quinton learned was named Ray Ray, was sixteen and had been working for Read for about three years now. He was Reads right hand man so Quinton figured that's why there was so much heat thrown at him because he checked him which apparently he rarely did.

*"So how did you start working for my pops?"* Quinton asked Read.

Read sat back against the couch. *"Aye Lil G, go to the kitchen and grab me a beer man. And tell Miss Donna to hook me up with some of them greens."*

*"Aight you got it."* The eager boy said as he left the room.

Read looked at Quinton and his appearance. His whole vibe gave off a good spirited church boy. He knew that he would have to keep his eye on him because he was blind to the world around him.

"I met your pops a few weeks after I moved here from New York. I had caught a charge upstate so my mom's sent me here to live with my aunt to try to get my life together and what not. I was on the corner one day tryna push some nickel bags when these dudes came up on me telling me I was in their spot. I was outnumbered and I mean shit I can handle my own but I ain't no stupid nigga ya feel me? So I pulled out my heat and had all them niggas on the ground and took all they shit. I told em it was my corner now. One nigga was on the end crying and shit and I don't even know where the nigga came from but, I heard somebody cock on me. I turn around and your pops is standing there with this glock in my face and I don't know why but I froze, and I ain't never froze on nobody in my life. He asked me who the fuck I was and snatched the gun out my hand. I told him I was new and was just tryna eat. Yo kid, I thought I was gonna die right there. But the nigga didn't cap my ass. I remember him yelling, 'you stupid ass nigga, you could've got your ass killed for some measly ass coins!' I told him what was some measly coins to him was fucking millions to a hungry nigga like me. So Bishop took me back to his trap and took me under his wing. He put me with the same crew I

34

*tried to rob and had me in charge of them niggas!"* he said laughing.

Lil G had come back in the room with the food and beer that Read had asked for. He sat down and listened as Read finished telling the story.

Read took a long sip of beer before he finished. *"I worked that crew and man, I worked my way up in the streets. Before long, Bishop had me recruiting new soldiers and I started making out of town trips for him. Everybody was so scared of this cat man. I was used to niggas skimming off the top to try to get them a little extra but, nobody ever did that to Bishop. He just had that respect like that man. The one time somebody did try to cross him, the nigga was never seen again. Bishop could touch you and not be near you ya feel me? He took care of all of us man. He made sure that I sent money to my mom's back home, and when my little shorty was born, he even bought her a nursery. Like he looked out for everybody."*

Quinton wouldn't believe that this was the same man that he called his father. Read seemed to have so much respect for him even though he didn't even acknowledge his own son. He was young, but he knew his mother was not Bishops main girl and she just happened to get pregnant. *Oh so he can go and take care of somebody else's baby but not his own,* He thought to himself. He kept his thoughts to himself because he didn't want to disrespect Read or taint his image.

*"Well he's definitely nothing like that now."* Quinton said. *"That almost seems like a whole nether person. My pops don't even let us talk about drugs much less sell it. He's all into the church now. Guess you never know a person."*

Read sat with the most serious expression. *"Your pops had some other shit going on outside of the drug shit. Now real talk, your pops was all about his money but, that nigga was in some fatal attraction shit. He was dating this bad ass chic named Anna and she was his main chic. Everybody knew it. But he like most niggas like to have his options too. He had this one chic named Tanya, your mama. Man Tanya had everybody wanting to holla at her. She was thick as hell."* He said smiling.

*"Man come on."* Quinton said agitated not wanting to think about

his mother in that way.

*"My bad my nigga."* Read said with a laugh. *"Well, Bishop started fucking with Tanya almost as hard as he was fucking with Anna. We kept telling that nigga to be careful because he was always up under her and everybody was starting to think that was his girl and shit. Then one day we started noticing that Tanya was a little heavy and everybody on the block said it was Bishops baby. We wanted to tell him that he was fucking up but, this was Bishop. I mean who the fuck was gonna check him? She disappeared and got ghost. Then one day Bishop came through telling us that Tanya had popped up at his and his girls crib with you and told him she wasn't gonna raise him by herself. So him and Anna was split for a while but he still took care of her. Every chance Anna got, she was coming at Tanya. I remember Tanya came over here one day to get some money from Bishop for you and Anna came out of nowhere. She was crazy man."*

Quinton sat with his eyebrows up in surprise at all that he was hearing. He didn't expect his father to say anything but his mother never told him any of this. *"I don't get it man.*

*What's that gotta do with him becoming a pastor?"* he asked confused.

Read sighed heavily not sure how he would take the next part. *"Well man basically, one day Anna showed up at the trap while Bishop was in the room playing with you. She pulled a gun out on you and Bishop and he starts screaming at her to calm down and relax and that he loves her. She told him that she was pregnant and didn't wanna have his baby because it wouldn't be his first born and shit. Yo son, I don't know what she was on B. It was some crazy shit. She turned the gun on herself and shot herself in the chest."*

Quinton sat straight up in his seat. He couldn't believe what he was hearing! His stepmother tried to kill herself? *"Man it fucked us all up, so I know it fucked him up. They rushed her to the hospital and she was in there forever man. She was in a coma and shit for like a month. The baby didn't make it. I remember coming to check on him and he looked me dead in my eyes and said that if God pulled her through, he would give all this shit up. I guess God believed him cause the next day, she woke up."*

38

Quinton sat in disbelief. *"So he just walked away?"* he asked.

*"Yea man."* Read answered. *"The next day, he gathered us all together, and told us he was giving it up. He said that God gave him a second chance in life through Anna. He split all his money he had made in the game between us and walked out. A lot of niggas took they money and blew through that shit on cars, clothes and bitches. But me, I took my shit, and turned it into this."* He said as he pointed at everything around him. *"Now the same niggas that was living lavish for a second, work for me."*

Quinton's mouth flew open. *"You mean to tell me that he gave away all the money he made? That's crazy man!"* he said.

Read shook his head in agreement. *"Yea man it is. Everybody thought the nigga had lost his mind or something B. But he was serious. So he gave up all his shit, and then him and Anna went to the courthouse and made it official. I know shorty was bugged for a minute over the whole baby thing but, Bishop made it clear he wasn't gonna abandon you."* A look of sadness came over his face. *"I saw him not too long after that. He was walking down the street with*

*Anna and I tried to speak to him but, he acted like he didn't even know me. I can't even get mad at him though. You gotta do what you can to take care of your fam. But I'm gonna always look out for him man. That's respect."*

Quinton took in everything that Read had told him. There had always been a funny relationship between him and Anna but, he could never put his finger on it as to why she treated him so cold. Traniece could do no wrong and was her pride and joy and although in public they were the perfect blended family, she really didn't communicate with him much except to tell him something his father needed him to do. Now it all started to make sense. He felt like Anna hated him and now he knew why.

Read took some weed out his pocket and rolled a blunt. *"You smoke?"* he asked laughing.

*"Nah man you cool. Go ahead."* Quinton responded trying to sound cool.

Read kept laughing. *"Man this ain't no after school special. Smoke some with your boy. Aint nobody gonna fuck with you."*

Quinton sat forward and took the blunt out of Reads hand. He took a puff from it and began to choke on it. Read sat back and stifled a laugh as he watched Quinton try to hit it again. *"Ay yo calm down son. You hit that shit too hard you gone be hurting."* He laughed.

Read took the blunt from Quinton and took a long drag of it before passing it to Lil G. Lil G took a drag and passed it back to Quinton. The three sat back getting high and Quinton listened to Read tell more stories of his father's past. From that day, Read became Quinton's hero and brother.

\*

*"The doors of the church are open."* Bishop said to his congregation as he stood on the pulpit bringing his sermon to a close. The congregation was swaying and shouting as the music continued to play. Quinton sent Read a text to let him know that he was on the way when Anna walked over to the ushers to assist Sister Watson when she caught the spirit, which she happened to do every week.

*Quinton: Yea. Still at the church house. Hopefully my pops wont trip.*
*Should be there in bout an hour.*

Quinton put his phone back in his pocket and went to go
collect the Bishops things off the pulpit like he did every Sunday.
Bishop had a thing about getting his family involved in church as
much as possible. Traniece stood at the front of the alter with the
rest of the youth lay speakers to welcome anyone that felt moved by
the sermon to join the church. Traniece was grinning from ear to
ear but she clearly wasn't paying attention to anything that was
going over.

Quinton looked over and saw that she was looking at
Robert, a boy that he had gone to school with. Robert was the nigga
that had everybody fooled. He was in church every Sunday with his
mama but was deep in the game almost as much as Read. Quinton
made it his mission to have a conversation with him, with Reads
help of course. His little sister and him were tight despite the fact
that the mothers couldn't stand each other. Out of everything that
the Bishop griped at him about, his bond with his sister was one he
took seriously. He caught her attention and quickly shot his eyes to

42

Bishop and Anna to let her know that she was being watched. She straightened up and began to pass out welcome cards to the guests that were coming up and leading them into the reception area.

The service ended and everyone started walking around and greeting one another, gossiping and catching up on the events that occurred in the week. Quinton rushed to the reception overflow area so that by the time his father got there he could be ready to go. He walked over to Traniece and whispered to her *"stay in here and don't leave."*, as he continued to walk by. She acknowledged him by shaking her head yes never breaking her conversation.

About twenty minutes later, Bishop and Anna walked in the room hand in hand greeting the guests as they neared. Quinton was trying his hardest to be patient but it seemed like everyone wanted to talk to Bishop that day. Quinton got an idea and decided to wait until Bishop was around the most individuals to ask if he could catch a ride. He sat back and made small chat with some of the other members and excused himself when he saw his opportunity.

*"Hey dad is it okay if I go ahead and head home? I got some*

*homework that I need to catch up on."* He said as politely as he could.

Bishop gave him a look that read *"Do I look stupid?"* to let him know he wasn't trying to hear any of Quinton's lies. *"Son we still have things tend to here so you can't just go running off."* He said.

*"I know dad. But, I've already closed down the sound booth, cleaned up your pulpit and cleaned the pews. I thought you wanted me to do my homework? You just gave me a two hour lecture on making sure I got my schoolwork done and how I needed to stop skipping school. Now you don't want me to go home and do what you were telling me to do in the first place?"* Quinton asked.

Bishop thought for a minute. He was about to tell him no and that he really hoped that he wasn't trying to pull one because he knew all the tricks in the book. But then he remembered what he had to deal with.

*"Okay son if you insist."* Bishop said. *"But take your sister with you. And I will have Brother David come by to check on you. I am going to take Anna for a dinner."* He said distracted.

Quinton noticed that his father was trying not to stare at a particular woman that was in the visiting area. One thing he and his father had in common was a weakness for was pretty girls with long legs. And this girl was definitely catching attention. Her calves made it appear as if she ran track they were so tight. Quinton was staring her down and oddly his father kept trying to turn away. *"You taking Anna to dinner?"* he asked to draw his attention away from the girl. *"What's wrong?"*

Bishop made sure to keep his thoughts separate from his relationship with Quinton. He didn't want him influenced by him negatively in any way. It was bad enough his son was already so easily influenced. He tried to let his son do his own thing because he was a boy and some lessons had to be learned the hard way, but at the same time he didn't want him being stupid either. He knew that Quinton was not planning on going home to do homework but that he wanted to go off with Read. He had no beef with Read; just what Read represented. He was a part of his past and he wanted to keep Quinton away from that as much as possible. He knew what Read was about and he needed Quinton to realize that before it was too late. He didn't want to keep such a tight grip on Quinton but he didn't know what else to do. He really didn't trust leaving Quinton alone at the house but he knew he also needed to smooth things over with Anna too before he got into too much trouble. At least Traniece will be there with him. *I know she will keep him out of trouble,* he thought to himself. He snapped back to attention when he heard Quinton calling his name.

*"Dad! Dad!"* Quinton said.

*"Oh sorry son I was thinking about something. Nothings the matter. I just want to have some alone time with her. With everything going on lately with the church, and the sick and shut in and you, I haven't really had time for her so, I wanted to at least treat her to dinner."* He answered. *"Now I'm about to go into this meeting so, grab your sister and head on home. She seems to be entertaining that young man over there and I can see Anna ready to burn a hole in the back of his head."* Bishop said with a chuckle.

Quinton turned around to see Traniece in the face of Robert and stifled back an angry expression. He definitely had to stop that shit and quick. She couldn't be discreet about it if she tried. She looked like a love sick little girl batting her eyes all in his face and flirting with him. *"Aight dad I will see you at the house in a few. Traniece!"* he yelled to get her attention.

Traniece jumped and rolled her eyes at Quinton. Bishop shook his head in frustration. *"Son, was that really necessary?"* he asked.

*"Well it got her away from him didn't it?"* he asked sarcastically as Traniece was quickly approaching.

*"Oh my gosh, really Q? That was so ghetto!"* Traniece hissed putting on a front. Traniece had her father completely fooled. She was just as bad as Quinton, only she knew how to save face in front of her daddy. In his eyes, she was his little angel. She wasn't all the way ratchet, but around the right people, she soon would be.

*"Man whatever. Come on, pops said I gotta take you with me."* Quinton said happy to be leaving.

*"And you two go straight home. No stops along the way you got that Quinton?"*, Bishop said to Quinton.

47

*"I got it pops."* Quinton said already walking off.

*"Bye daddy."* Traniece said kissing her daddy on the cheek and walking off with her brother.

Bishop watched the two walk out the room and thought about how he worried over Quinton's behavior and worried about Traniece pure innocence and being naïve to the outside world. *"Lord give me strength."* He said.

\*

**Chapter Two**

Quinton and Traniece walked through the door of their five bedroom, 3 bathroom home in Buckhead. They had been living in Buckhead for over ten years. Bishop moved them completely out of College Park when he gave his life to God. They weren't living the lavish life, but they were doing better than most. Quinton had a Nissan Maxima that his father was taking away every two seconds because he was always grounded. He cut the alarm on as he and his sister walked into the house. Traniece had her cell phone in her hand and her thumbs were busy texting. Quinton, not really caring, went upstairs to his room to change clothes while she went into the kitchen. A few minutes later he came back down in some jeans, a white tee, and some sneakers. He walked into the kitchen to find Traniece sitting on a stool and texting drinking a soda.

*"Hey I'm bout to roll out with Read for a little bit. Pops said that he was taking your mom out to eat or whatever after his meeting so I should be good for a few hours. If he calls and asks, tell him I had to go see my mom's about something and I will be back. But just call*

*me if he says he on the way or something like that aight?*" he told his sister.

"*Aight.*" She said never looking up from her phone.

Quinton paused before he walked out the kitchen door. "*Aye who you texting anyway? You ain't put that phone down since you got in the car.*" He said.

"*Don't worry about who it is.*" She said. "*It ain't you. Dang do you see me all in your business tryna figure out what you doing? No. So, let me handle mine.*" She answered.

Quinton walked over to her and snatched her phone out her hand.

"*Q what the hell?!*" she yelled at him trying to take her phone back. Quinton held her back with his hand and looked at her phone with his other to see that she was texting Robert.

"*Yo I know this ain't the nigga that was just in your face a second ago.*" Quinton said angrily. "*You know damn well pops and your momsgonna kick your ass when they find out what that nigga* do." He said. Traniece was still struggling to get her phone back from him

"You act like you don't do the same damn thing Quinton, now give me my phone!" she yelled at him slapping at him.

Quinton threw her phone on the counter and grabbed her by the arm. "I'm serious Niecey. I ain't tryna deal with this bullshit right now." He said. "This nigga is full of shit and he ain't gonna do shit but try to fuck and then move on to the next shit. Don't let that little church boy shit fool you." He said.

"What church boy shit? He's in the church every Sunday with his mama and daddy." Traniece said foolishly.

Quinton looked at her like she was completely stupid and tapped her forehead with his finger. "Think about it Niecey! I'm in church every Wednesday, Thursday and Sunday and I damn sure ain't no angel! You think just cause the nigga in church that he ain't living foul? Man please! Them be the main ones. Stay away from him Niecey, I ain't playing. Cause I will fuck his ass up." He said serious.

Traniece was fuming but she wasn't going to argue with

him. She kept her mouth shut and went back to sit down. *"Can I have my phone please?"* she said with an attitude. *"I can't text you when daddy is coming back if you keep my phone."*

Quinton rolled his eyes giving her the phone that she couldn't seem to live without. *"I'm serious. I ain't tryna tell you how to do you but, it ain't gonna be with some fucking street hustler."* He said as he walked out the door.

*"I don't know who the hell he think he talking to. He ain't my daddy."* She said to herself. She picked up her phone and called him.

*"Wassup sexy?"* he answered after a few rings.

*"So.... What's this my brother is talking bout you hustling and stuff? What you sell drugs?"* Traniece asked with an attitude.

*"Hold up. First of all, don't be calling me tryna jump down my throat. I don't know who you think this is but, I ain't one of these little high school boys."* He said into the phone.

*"Whatever. All I wanna know is where the hell my brother hear that you hustling and shit Rob? You know I can't be talking to*

you if that's how you get down. You know my pops be watching me like a hawk!" Traniece said.

She heard him sigh on the phone and heard a door close. "First of all shawty your brother don't even know me. You see me all the time so the fact that you believe him is stupid. Now do I hang around some people that hustle? Yes. But does that make me a hustler? No. So dead all that noise you bringing." He said.

Traniece didn't know what to believe. She was really feeling Rob but she knew her brother wouldn't just make some stuff out the clear blue. Maybe he just saw him hanging out with some guys that do hustle, she thought to herself. He did say he hung around guys that was hustling and slanging. "I'm sorry.", was all she could say.

"Look shawtyI'm feeling you and all but I ain't about all that drama and accusing stuff. If I wanted to talk to somebody like that I would go mess with one of these birds on the corner. But I was talking to you because I thought you were different than that." He said.

Traniece started smiling. *"So you tryna talk to me? Really?"* she asked naïve.

*"Yea. But not if you gonna act like that. I can't be telling everybody I'm dating you and you acting like some bird. It's bad enough you a PK. I'm already gonna have people in my business."* He told her.

*"What's a PK?"* Traniece asked.

She heard him laugh on the other line. *"A PK is a preacher's kid shawty. And no offense but just cause your daddy is a pastor don't mean that he was one all his life. I done heard stories about him. Correct me if I'm wrong but, didn't he used to sell and hustle back in the day?"* he asked her already knowing the answer. He wasn't stupid, and he knew what he was doing. But he couldn't let her know that yet. His boys would forever give props if they knew he had gotten the Bishops daughter on his team.

*"Yea my daddy USED to sell."*, she emphasized. *"But that was before I was even born. I know all about that. As much as my father is into the word, he ain't turning back. And you shouldn't be*

*scared of him. Now Quinton on the other hand....”*

Robert was on the other end of the phone trying not to let her hear that he was getting angry. *“I ain’t scared of Quinton neither. That’s the one ya need to be questioning right there.”* He said calm. *“I heard that he be kicking it with that dude Read. And I know he be hustling. Somebody told me he got a trap house and your brother be in there all the time. You grilling him like you grilling me?”* he asked.

Traniece was starting to get frustrated. *“Okay well dang first of all calm down. I heard something so I just wanted to know. If you heard something about me, wouldn’t you wanna know about it? Wouldn’t you ask me since you so called tryna get at me?”* she asked.

*“Yea. But you ain’t gotta come at me like that. That’s what I’m talking bout.”* He said to her.

*“Ok so, I apologized for that so....let’s move on. We got stuff cleared up now I’m good.”* She said as she began walking up the stairs to her bedroom. She walked into her room, closing her door behind her and laying on her bed. *“So we cool?”* she asked sweetly.

*“Yea we cool.”* Robert answered. *“But I’m gonna have to hit you back*

*cause I'm about to go run and help my mom's with some stuff."*

*"Okay."* She pouted. *"Call me later?"* she asked hopeful.

*"Yea aight."* He said hanging up.

Traniece hit the end button on her phone and sat back. *"Quinton don't know what he's talking about. Robert is nothing like that."* She grabbed her bear, hugged it close, and drifted off to sleep smiling.

*

Quinton walked into the trap house that Read had in Bankhead. He looked around the living room and saw a bunch of young boys playing video games. He shook his head because he walked right in without them giving him a second look. He knew Read must not be there because when he was they didn't do a thing without his say so. He walked into the kitchen to make sure that everyone was going as it was supposed to. He saw a young looking girl at the table cutting dope. His eyebrows shot up because even though she looked young, the girl was bad. He looked her up and down and the first thing he noticed was that she had a tremendous ass. Her legs were long and thighs were nice and firm. She looked very athletic to Quinton but he didn't want to say anything just yet. Her face was what really stood out because her skin seemed flawless. From what he could see, she had green eyes which really made her stand out. He knew she was probably getting guys left and right as good as she looked so he decided not to give her too much attention and let her show herself.

After being satisfied that everything was going as it should in the kitchen, he walked around to one of the bedrooms. He peeked inside he cracked door to see that there were 2 guys fucking a girl the girl was on her knees bent over getting hit from the back while sucking the other boy's dick. He's surprised there was no one there with popcorn watching from the sound of skin slapping. He smirked and walked on back to the living room. The guys were still sitting on the couch playing video games. One of the boys was Lil G. He looked up to see Quinton staring at them.

*"Wassup PK? When did you get here?"* he asked walking over and dapping him up.

Quinton looked over at the group and dapped him back. *"I been here for a minute man. I walked right past ya'll like ten minutes ago and done walked through damn near the whole house man. None of ya'll niggas saw anything?"* he asked Lil G.

Lil G tried not to look too embarrassed but he knew Quinton was right. He tried to laugh it off but he knew Quinton was right. They were supposed to be alert at all times for anybody that came near the trap. No one really tried Read but still, the fact that Quinton was able to walk into the house and no one say anything didn't look good.

*"My bad man. We were playing that new Madden and I guess we was all caught up."* He told him.

Ray Ray was sitting amongst the group of boys playing video games on the couch and was listening to the conversation between Lil G and Quinton while still playing the video game. *"What the fuck you apologizing to this nigga for? He ain't Read."* He said never looking up from the game. The rest of the guys got real quiet so that they could watch the outcome.

*"What the fuck you say man?"* Quinton asked trying to keep his patience. Ever since he met Ray Ray from the day he came up the walkway, he had been trying him. Quinton was trying not to pop off on him because he was Reads soldier and he respected Read to not fight over what seemed to be petty jealousy, but he was starting to really piss him off and he needed to check him soon otherwise he was going to keep trying him.

*"I didn't fucking stutter nigga. You heard me."* Ray Ray said still playing the video game. *"Don't be coming in here acting like you run shit. You just in here cause of your daddy nigga."*

Quinton's blood was starting to boil. He knew if he hit him, there was a strong possibility that Ray Ray would play dirty and use something other than his fists. But he was two seconds from throwing respect out the door and whooping his ass! *"Look my nigga, I don't give a fuck what you do. I'm telling you, ya'll fucking slacking off on this security shit cause a nigga just walked the fuck up in the house without so much as a second glance. You supposed to be Read top dog nigga and you over here playing some fucking video game dog."* Quinton walked closer to Ray Ray so that there would be no confusion. *"And as far as why I'm here, don't worry bout why the fuck I'm here. What you need to be worried about is who the fuck else is here."* He said with all seriousness.

Ray Ray stood up when he saw Quinton coming towards him. *"Like I said before nigga, the only reason niggas is tolerating your ass is cause of your daddy. But I don't give a fuck. You don't run shit in here. I do."* He said inches away from Quinton.

*"Oh really?"* Everyone turned around to see Read standing there. Immediately everyone started to try to clean up and act as if nothing was going on. Quinton and Ray Ray were still in standoff mode but now Quinton was grinning.

*"See nigga if you was running shit, you would've seen Read come in here five minutes ago. But you were too busy playing Madden right? Oh but you run shit."* He said with a smirk. He knew Ray Ray wanted to swing on him but he wouldn't dare with Read standing there.

Read walked to the center of the room where Ray Ray and Quinton stood. He stood beside Quinton facing Ray Ray. *"So that I am clear, I run all this shit. If any muthafucka is unsure of who is in*

*charge, it is the nigga that pays you, that feeds you, and that's me.*

*And I don't know who the fuck told you otherwise, but I will always*

*run shit. And as far as I'm concerned Ray Ray, you're done."* Read

said stone faced.

Ray Ray turned to Read in disbelief. *"Read man, what the fuck?*

*You gone listen to this nigga?"* he said pointing at Quinton. *"Bruh*

*come on man we been cool for years, you know I got your back man.*

*A nigga was just chillin for a minute man. My bad I didn't know you*

*had come in man."*

Read stood there listening to him not fazed. *"Everybody out*

*except for me, Quinton and Ray Ray."* He said, and immediately, the

room cleared. Lil G was one of the last ones to walk out. *"Lil G, post*

*up outside."*

*"You got it."* Lil G said and walked across the room to the front door

standing on his post.

*"Now to keep from further embarrassing you in front of*

*everyone more than you already are, I'm telling you that I no longer need you. Dawg you been slipping for a while. All this shit ain't sudden. I been watching. Just cause I ain't in the trap all the time don't mean that I don't know what's going on."* Read walked over to the TV and picked up a flower pot. He pulled a small black piece out of it. *"Dawg I been recording you for weeks and you know you been fucking up. I walked the fuck up in here but you was so into some fucking game that you could've just hit the pause button on that you didn't even see it. I don't need nobody like that on my team man. I need soldiers. Quinton didn't get you bounced, you got yourself bounced."*

Ray Ray stood with his jaw clenched wanting to beat the shit out of Quinton but Read would've blocked him before he even got close. Quinton stood not sure of what to say. But he kept his eyes on Ray Ray just in case.

*"So, all these years and I'm out? Just like that?"* Ray Ray asked.

*"You made it like that bruh. But I ain't gonna just leave you hanging."* Read went to the safe on the wall and opened it pulling out $10,000. He threw the banded stack of money at Ray Ray.

*"Consider this.....severance."* He said and walked away.

Ray Ray caught the stack, looked over at Quinton and Read, shook his head and walked out the door. Quinton had a feeling it wasn't over though.

Quinton stood there replaying everything that happened in front of him. When he saw that Ray Ray wasn't coming back, he walked into the kitchen to find Read at the table.

*"Read man what the fuck? I wasn't tryna start no shit or get that nigga kicked out man. I was just tryna look out when I saw that wasn't nobody guarding the shit. I ain't tryna fuck up a nigga paper."* He said.

Read looked up from the table and laughed. *"Nigga what the fuck I just tell him out there? You didn't fuck up that nigga paper. He fucked his own shit up. Hell he knew what the fuck he was supposed to do but he let his fucking ego get in the way. I can't have anybody like that on my team dog. And besides, I gave that nigga some paper to where he can be on his feet for a minute."* He said as he walked over to the fridge to fix him something to eat.

Quinton still looked uneasy. *"Yea but what if that nigga try to get at you?"* he asked concerned.

Read burst out laughing. *"Man please! That nigga ain't stupid. I will know about that shit before the nigga is even finished planning the shit. Don't stress that shit. He good."* He answered him nonchalant.

Quinton was amazed that Read wasn't fazed by letting go of someone that had been down with him from day one. *"So what the hell you gonna do man? Lil G ain't gonna be able to hold down all them niggas by himself."* He said.

*"I already got it handled. I got somebody."* Read told him while he stuffed his face.

*"Who?"* he asked.

Read looked up and pointed. *"You."*

Quinton's eyebrows shot up. *"Me? I don't know everything about this man. I'm not here like that and besides, you already know my pops will flip the hell out if he even thinks I'm within a block of this place my nigga."* He said serious.

Read got up and walked over to Quinton. *"Look man, you'll be cool. I ain't just gone throw your ass out there with no knowledge of what the hell you doing. I don't run my joint like that. I got you. That is, if you willing to handle it. I don't need no more niggas that do one thing in front of me and then another behind my back."*

*"Dawg I feel you but, I don't know. I gotta think about some shit like this. I mean you my nigga all day but, I ain't no thug man. I don't know if I'm built for this shit."* Quinton said confused.

*"If I didn't feel like you was built for it, I wouldn't ask."* Read said still sitting and eating.

*"I don'tknow man, this is some stuff I gotta think about."* Quinton said as he sighed heavily running his hand across his head.

Read shook his head in agreement. *"Aight. I'll give you that. Just think on it and holla at me. Don't wait too long though. Gotta have somebody to take over and soon."* He said.

Quinton shook his head and felt his phone vibrate. He pulled his phone out and saw a text message from his sister.

*Lil Sis 7:57pm: Mom and dad are home!*

*Quinton 7:58pm: Damn. How long they been there?*

*Lil Sis 7:59pm: I don't know, I fell asleep. My bad.*

*Quinton 7:59pm: WTF?! Are you serious? Aight I'm on the way.*

*"Aye man I gotta go. My pops is home and I'm supposed to be studying and Niecey was supposed to text me before he got there but fell the hell asleep."* Quinton told Read.

*"Damn that's fucked up. Bishop got you on a leash like that? It's just now 8 o'clock."* Read said.

*"I know. Man I ain't even tryna hear this shit when I get home. All he gonna do is nag then Anna gonna jump in and say how I'm disrespecting the house like I'm some guest or something. Dawg I can't wait to get out of there."* Quinton said.

Read shook his head back and forth. *"I can't believe you are eighteen and still got like a curfew and shit."* He started laughing.

*"This is like some Family Matters type shit PK."* He stopped laughing when he saw the look on Quinton's face. *"But seriously though, if you tryna get out like that, I mean you can always crash at my spot. It ain't the Ritz or nothing but, you ain't gotta be up under your pops thumb."* He said.

*"I appreciate that. Hell I might as well sit and chill and eat since I'm already in trouble anyway."* Quinton said as he walked to the refrigerator to fix him something to eat. The two sat down and ate, and drank and talked about their hustle until almost midnight.

*

Quinton walked into his house at 12:37 am trying to be as quiet as possible. He figured maybe if he snuck upstairs, he could somehow trick his father into thinking that he had been in the house the entire time and was just somewhere where they couldn't find him. He slowly walked up the stairs making sure not to make any noise. He got to his bedroom door to open and find his father and stepmother sitting on his bed.

*"Hello son. Nice of you to finally come home."* Bishop said.

Quinton stood quiet not saying anything. He already knew he was about to get the "Be more responsible" speech and get grounded. He leaned up against the wall to look his father in the eye and prepare for all he was about to say.

*"So where were you?"* Bishop asked his son.

*"I was at the library studying."* Quinton quickly responded.

Anna sat next to Bishop shaking her head in disbelief.

*"Really Quinton? Is that the best you could come up with? Studying?"* she asked him.

Bishop raised his hand to silence Anna.

*"It's okay honey. I got it."* He said. Anna looked at him and rolled her eyes. Quinton saw this and smirked at his father checking his stepmother in front of him. *"Son I really don't know what you were smirking about. You and I both know you weren't at the library. You walk in here way after your curfew in baggy jeans and looking like one of these thugs on the corner, and there is not as much as a book in your hand. And I can just about guarantee that*

any library will have cameras and will not be open this late. So, to lie and say you were at the library? Not smart son because you have no proof whatsoever. And even in the slightest chance that you did, I specifically told you not to leave the house and to come straight home and stay there. And what do I find when we return? Your sister here alone and your behind is out doing God knows what with God knows whom!" he shouted.

"Calm down Byron." Anna told him. She stood to her feet and stepped closer to Quinton. "We don't want to wake up Traniece. Look Quinton, you may not like the way things are here, and I know you think that your father and I are just trying to punish you. Now I know I'm not your mother, and I'm not trying to take her place, but this is our house and you need to respect that. This family has gone through too much and your father just doesn't want to see you going down the road that he did. It may seem like we don't know what's going on to you, but we know everything that you are doing. You don't think that we didn't know that you were in that drug house tonight? Quinton your father is a leader in the neighborhood who has many followers just ready to tell him what they see. You have to live *up to a certain standard because of who he is."* She said pointing to Bishop.

Quinton got heated when she said that. *"And that's the problem! I have to live up to his standards and can't breathe or do anything because of you pops!"* he said addressing his father. *"I'm not the Bishop, you are! But I can't do anything. I'm 18 years old and still have a curfew. I can't hang out with friends because all people gonna do is run back and tell my father. I didn't ask for this shit!"* Quinton snapped. Before he knew what happened, his father had jumped up and slammed him against the wall.

*"I don't know who you think you are talking to."* Bishop said through gritted teeth, *"But you are my son, in my house and you will not talk to me like that ever again. Do I make myself clear?"* he said.

Quinton stood staring his father eye to eye with his jaw clenched tight.

*"Yes sir."* He answered him.

*"Good. Now sit down."* Bishop demanded his son.

Quinton walked over to his chair and sat down while Bishop stood next to Anna who was now at the doorway.

*"Now look, I know you are eighteen and want to have fun and do your own thing. But while you live in this house, and so long as we pay for the roof over your head, the food that you eat, and the clothes that you wear, you will abide by our rules. I don't expect you to follow in my footsteps because you are your own man. But what I do expect Quinton Jeron White, is for you to respect this house and the people in it. I shouldn't have to worry if you are at home when I tell you to be and should be able to trust you in doing what's right son. Bottom line. If you don't like it, as you keep mentioning, you are 18. You can go out into the real world, and get a job and pay your own bills. Then you can do whatever you want to do. But until that day comes, you will do as I say. Now it's late. Go to bed and we'll finish talking about this in the morning. Come on Anna."* Bishop said as he opened the door to walk out. *"Good night son."*

Bishop closed the door and Quinton let out a loud huff. *I can't take this shit anymore,* he thought to himself. He thought about what his father said. He was right, he paid the bills and Quinton had it good. He considered getting a job and saving up to leave but he knew that would take forever and he was ready to get out from his father's watch as soon as possible. He thought about what Read asked him to do in working for him. *He did say I could crash with him*, he thought. *Hell I may not have my own space, but at least then I ain't gotta worry about hearing a bunch of bullshit about what I am doing with my life.* He pulled his phone out and called Read.

*"Yo PK what up?"* Read answered.

*"Hey man. Dealing with the same ole same ole. Pops went off when I got home. Man he was sitting in my room."* He said.

*"Damn son. That's that fuck shit. So what you gonna do?"* Read asked.

Quinton hesitated for a moment. *"Does that offer still stand for me to handle the soldiers?"* he asked in almost a whisper.

*"Yea man. I got you. You serious about doing this though? I ain't got time for no ABC Family drama man."* He said.

Quinton laughed at his sarcasm. *"Nah man I'm serious. I gotta do me man. I gotta get up out this house."*

*"Well like I said son my spot is open to you if you want. Just let a nigga now when."* Read told him.

*"Aight come scoop me in like an hour."* Quinton told him.

*"Oh you serious?"* Read asked.

*"Yea man. If I'm gonna go, it needs to be tonight. He should be sleep by then. All I gotta do is throw some stuff in a bag and I'm ready. Meet me down the street in like an hour."* Quinton instructed him.

*"Aight cool. I'll hit you in a few."* Read said.

    *"Aight one."* Quinton hung up the phone. He grabbed his duffle bag from under his bed and threw some clothes in there. He took his shoe box he had stashed in his closet that held a few hundred bucks he had been saving and put it in his wallet. As he was packing, he saw a picture of his sister. He smiled at the picture of him and her at the Six Flags theme park. Niecey was the only person he hated to leave but, he knew he couldn't take it anymore. He sat down at his desk and began to write.

*I had to get out of here. I'm not far though. I will be straight but I can't continue to live like a prisoner in dad's house. I love you lil knuckle head girl. Be good. And remember what I told you. I'm keeping my eye on you even when I ain't around. Tell pops and your mom's I'm sorry but, I gotta be my own man. I know this will be hard for you but I am still your big brother and still here for you. If you need me, you know how to reach me. I'll call you in a few days.*

*Love, Q*

Quinton grabbed his duffle bag, cut his light off and slowly crept down the stairs leaving his house and family. As he walked down the sidewalk, he turned around and looked at his house one last time before walking to Reads car.

\*

## Chapter Three

Quinton sat in his apartment drinking a beer and counting money from one of the soldiers that had come in to turn in his bank for the week. Six months had passed since he had left his father's house and he wasn't looking back. The nerdy little church boy that everyone knew died that night and "Q" was born. Gone were the slacks and dress shirts. Quinton changed his attire completely. He wore baggy jeans, Tim's, and a wife beater that showed off his broad shoulders and muscular arms.

Ever since he left home, Quinton was able to do what he wanted. He worked out every day to keep fit and in shape, had gotten a few pieces to wear around his neck to show off what he had saved up, and even got his own place. It didn't hurt that he was a looker, just like his father. At 6'4, Quinton definitely got the ladies attention. He had girls throwing themselves at him almost on a daily basis. His chocolate skin was flawless, and he had on deep dimple in his right cheek. When he smiled, you saw nothing but straight white teeth. Quinton was but short of an Adonis.

Now six months later, Q and Read ran the streets. Read was more-so in the streets but Q had his back on the inside. Q sat in the one bedroom apartment that he leased and loved it. All the soldiers answered to him when it came to turning in money and getting inventory. He still went to school and was still making the grades he needed to pass, and was graduating in a month. He just didn't have to hear his father's nagging. Everyone, including his mother tried to get him to go back home except his father. He saw his sister Niecey all the time at school and they were still close as ever. If he could just keep her away from Robert he would be straight. It was like she was slow when it came to him but smart any other time. Q had a conversation with him and told him he didn't trust him but, once again Robert pulled the good boy act.

Quinton now sat in his living room counting the money while the young soldier stood in front of him. He put the money the boy gave him in stacks in a shoe box and put it in his safe he had put into the wall. He didn't have much to look at in the apartment so as not to draw attention to himself since he was only 18, but the few things that were in there was his safe, and his secret compartment in his floorboards that held some of Reads stash and guns. He closed his safe and gave the boy a small duffle bag. *"Aight. Watch your surroundings kid. The block is hot lately."*

*"Got you Q."* the boy said.

The boy walked out the apartment and a young girl came in. Tierra was the girl from the trap house that Quinton had first seen six months ago. He didn't holler at her until a few months ago but ever since then, she had been his main chick. Quinton had spent the last six months smashing girls left and right and had made quite a reputation for himself. He still smashed the random birds in the streets but Tierra knew he wasn't going anywhere. She walked in showing off her figure in a red spaghetti strap dress with a gold chain around her neck with the letter "Q". Her hair was pulled into a high ponytail on top of her head with a few wisps of her hanging down.

*"Hey babe."* She said as she walked in and kissed him before heading to the kitchen to get a drink out of the refrigerator. She came back into the living room with her drink and sat down on the

couch cutting the television on.

Quinton shook his head as she sat entertained by Love and Hip Hop New York re-runs. He hated those shows but it seemed like that's all she watched. He honestly thought VH1 was the only channel that existed to her. *"Babe you know its other stuff you can watch on T.V. besides that mess right?"* he asked her.

She turned to him smiling and said *"I know. But this stuff is funny. I mean it ain't real or anything but, it's funny to watch. K. Michelle is taking over New York, and this chic Amina is like another Joseline Hernandez. All these side bitches getting wifed up. That is some trifling shit bae."*

Quinton chuckled and went back to stacking up the money. To hear her talk, she knew these people personally. *"Whatever you say. Did you go to the trap today?"* he asked. Ever since they had been kicking it, he had Read find her another job outside of working in the trap. He didn't want to have her so close to him since he was over the trap now.

*"Yea. Read and the crew was there. They looked pissed when I*

*was there. These two new soldiers was looking like they were going to get they ass beat though cause they stuff was short. Oh and Read told me to tell you to call him when you finished cause he needed you to meet up with him.*" She said as she turned back to the show.

"*Aight cool.*" Quinton said. He closed the safe and walked over to the couch where Tierra sat. "*In the mean time, why don't you come over here and show me some Love and Hip Hop.*" He asked her.

Tierra smiled, getting up and sitting on his lap facing him. "*Show you some love huh? Mmmmhow's this?*" she asked as she nibbled on his ear. She knew all his hot spots and sex with Tierra was the bomb. Quinton smashed other bitches just because he felt like he could but he knew that nobody came close to his girl.Before he knew it, she was getting on her knees in front of him and pulling his dick out. Quinton closed his eyes and sat back sighing. This girl's head game was phenomenal. She could get whatever she wanted and whenever when it came to her doming him up. He put his hand on the back of her head and guided her head up and down.

*"Yea baby. Just like that. Taste daddy dick."* He instructed her.

She began sucking and slurping faster making Quinton's toes curl in his boots. Not wanting to come yet, he picked her up off her knees and laid her on the couch. Taking his pants off, he raised her dress up to reveal that she wasn't wearing any underwear. *"Really?"* he asked her.

She smiled seductively at him. *"Well I kind of figured you would want some so I thought why not just take em off ahead of time?"*

Quinton smiled showing his dimple and entered her slowly making her gasp for air. Her pussy was the perfect fit to him. She was the perfect girl. She knew how to hustle and make her own paper, she didn't ask her nigga for shit, even though Quinton was glad to give it, and she knew how to put it down in the bedroom. He began to stroke her long and slow listening to her purr and moan. She was whispering his name while grabbing at his back from the good feeling that he was giving her.

*"Feel good baby?"* he asked her.

*"Yes baby, yes!"* she said clawing deeper into his skin. *"Oh God I'm*

*about to come!"* she moaned.

Quinton began to fuck her harder moving the couch as he thrust into her. *"Well come on then. Come on that dick so I can bust all down your throat."* He growled. He felt her coming on his dick making him thrust harder. He pulled out before he lost control and she sat up taking him in her mouth. He let out a loud grunt as he came all in her mouth. She drank his seed greedily and swallowed it all draining him of every drop.

*"Damn."* Quinton said as he pulled out and pulled his pants back up. It was moments like that when the sex was just that damn good; he couldn't get all of his clothes off. He walked to the bathroom to turn the shower water on. He stripped himself down and got in, lathering himself with Oak for Men by Bath and Body Works. He wasn't a fan of the women's store but Tierra had got it for him so he wore it just for her. As much as he hated to admit it, the stuff smelled good. Plus it drove Tierra crazy. He washed his body and left the shower running for Tierra since he knew she would be coming in right behind him. He went to his bedroom, grabbed a pair of boxers out the dresser drawer and put on the

matching Oak for Men body lotion. He dressed in a pair of black Roca wear jeans, white tee, and a black Gucci shirt unbuttoned. He put on a white gold chain and his rings. He heard Tierra getting into the shower and grabbed his keys and wallet.

*"Hey I'm about to head over to Read's."* he told her. She peeked her head out of the shower curtain. *"Don't be in here watching them damn reality shows all day. I'll be back in a few."*

*"Aight baby. I may head over there after I take a nap. I'm a little tired."* She said yawning.

*"Uh huh. Wore that ass out huh?"* Quinton said looking at her soapy body in the shower.

She laughed and went back to her shower. *"Boy get out and go make that money. Ain't nobody worried about you."* She said as she closed the curtain back.

Quinton smirked, checked himself in the mirror and walked out to meet up with his boy.

\*

Quinton drove down Flat Shoals Road in College Park. He was pushing a new whip Read had bought him a few months ago. His father had his car towed when he left so he was bumming rides with Read for a while. But Read looked out and paid for his Beamer in cash since he was under 21. Quinton was hesitant about it at first but Read had assured him he had more than earned it. Especially since not even a month after he was put in charge of the soldiers at the trap, they caught one of the boys trying to skim money off the top. Quinton wasn't sure what happened to him but, knowing Read, he was dead somewhere in some ditch where he couldn't be identified. So to thank him, Read bought him the car.

He cruised down the street with his windows down, bumping Future's "I Won". He started rapping along to the song as he pulled up to the stoplight.

*"I just want to take you out and show you off*

*You already know that you the perfect one*

*Girl when I'm with you, feel like a champion*

*Ever since I got with you I feel like I done won me a trophy*

*Trophy, I won me a trophy*

*A trophy, I won me a trophy*

*Trophy, I won me a trophy*

*A trophy"*

He looked over to the car beside him where he saw it was full of girls, one of whom he recognized from school. She looked up to see him and gave him a smile.

*"Maxine right?"* he asked as he leaned over.

*"Yea."* She answered nonchalantly. *"How are you Quinton?"*

The other girls were in the car all smiling and throwing Quinton looks that said he could get it.

*"I'm good shawty. Not as good as you look though."* He said flashing her his winning smile. *"Where you ladies headed to?"* he asked.

*"To the mall."* One of the girls in the back responded. Maxine gave the girl an irritated look. *"What? He asked!"* The girl told her.

Quinton smiled at the girl's attitude. *"That's wassup. Maxine why don't you come over here and take a ride with me?"* he asked her as the other girls in the car started smiling and growing wide eyed. The light changed to green and Maxine looked at it and smirked.

*"Sorry, gotta go."* She said as she rolled up the window. Her friend that was driving the car shook her head and eased the car out into traffic.

Not feeling her response, Quinton sped up and pulled in front of their car. Every time she tried to switch lanes, he would cut over to prevent her from gaining speed on him. The girl blew her horn at him in frustration. Quinton steered his car to the right and looked out the window at Maxine who was sitting on the passenger side.

*"So you gonna pull over or what?"* he asked.

Maxine said something to her friend and the girl put her turning signal on. Quinton smiled and followed. The two pulled over and he got out the car. He walked over and he could see the girls primping themselves through the windshield of the car. He approached the passenger side and opened the car door for Maxine to allow her opportunity to get out. Maxine looked up at him as if he had a third eye.

*"Ummm I'm not getting out this car."* She told him. *"You can tell me whatever it is that you have to say from right there."*

*"Damn slim you can't step out the car for your boy? You got me out here in the middle of Main Street looking like something out of some movie or something. Yo I will lay down in front of the car and sit until you get out."* He told her. She continued looking at him like she was crazy. *"Don't believe me?"* he questioned as he walked towards the front of her friends Ford Taurus.

*"Girl you better get out this car. Hurry up, I'm tryna go shopping and ya'll playing."* He friend fussed at her.

Maxine huffed a sigh. *"Fine. I'm getting out the car."* She said as she stepped out the car. Quinton walked back around as he looked at her walking towards him in a black halter jumper with gold accessories. She had micro braids in her head that were in small curls and she wore no makeup with the exception of lip gloss accentuating her small face and even skin tone. Quinton looked at her in amazement. He didn't let it show on his face but, he was really feeling her and he wanted her. He had Tierra, but he didn't feel like he did with Maxine. He would see her in the halls in school but she didn't even acknowledge him, so he definitely wanted to seize this opportunity.

*"So what's up beautiful? You looking nice and cute."* He told her.

Maxine tried not to show her disgust. *"So is this why you were driving like a maniac? So you could tell me I look cute?"* she rolled her eyes at him.

*"I mean damn calm down shawty. I was just trying to make you smile. You don't have to be so mean sweetheart."* He told her smoothly.

*"Quinton, what is it that you want? I mean I'm not trying to be funny but, I really don't have time for this. What you want my number or something? What? Let me guess, you and your girlfriend broke up?"* she laughed when she saw the surprised look on his face. *"Oh you didn't think I knew that you had a girlfriend? Oh trust I know that and a lot more about you Quinton."* She said smartly.

Quinton leaned against his car and listened to her without any expression. He knew she was right and he knew everybody knew Tierra was his girl. She made that known to any and everyone so that he couldn't do dirt. Not all the girls gave a damn though. Some just wanted to say that they had a piece of Quinton White and he was happy to oblige. Maxine was different though. He saw her as a challenge. He took this opportunity to try to smooth things over.

*"Well first off, I know I got a girl. Like I said, I'm just trying to make one of the hottest Georgia peaches smile. And please, call me Q. Only my parents call me Quinton."* He said.

*"Well Quinton, if you are trying to make me smile, you did. Now can I leave or, are you going to try to throw yourself off a bridge?"* she asked him sarcastically.

Quinton threw his hands up in mock surrender. *"Alright. You win. I hope you have a good day sexy. I'll see you around."* He winked as he watched her walk back to the car with her awaiting friends.

She stopped and turned back towards him. *"Oh and by the way, tell your father I said hello and we will see him in Bible study."*

She smirked and got in the car.

Quinton shook his head slowly as he watched them drive off. He got back in his car and drove off to meet Read while thinking of her.

*

Quinton pulled up to a white and red house on Old National Road. The house was one of the nicest in the middle of a run-down neighborhood and to the locals it was the trap. Quinton knew the cops had been watching Read but, he had several spots in Atlanta so, they never had anything solid to pin on him. Quinton had Read add on some features to the house in the last six months so that if the cops ever did raid the place, they would be covered. He did most of the construction during the day and had people outside repairing the house and fixing what looked like normal parts of the house that have had wear and tear. What was not seen were the workers on the inside of the house that were digging an underground tunnel that Read could use in the event that he needed to run from the law. The tunnel was about 2 miles wide that went right to the Atlanta MARTA station.

Quinton had also set up an account under a fake name through one of his connects at the bank so if Read needed to run, he would have easy access to money. One thing about Quinton being popular with the ladies is that they would do anything to get a piece of him. So when needed, Quinton took full advantage. Being a part of Reads Soldiers definitely had its benefits because before, he never would have had the same confidence to talk to girls the way he did now. His connect at the bank might as well had been old enough to be his mama.

Quinton got out the car and walked up the walkway to the house. He saw Lil G sitting on the porch texting on his cell phone while keeping an eye out. Lil G had really stepped it up ever since they got rid of Ray Ray. He was one of Quinton's head Soldiers under him. Even though he was extremely young, Quinton could tell that he had been through a lot. Lil G stood up when he saw Quinton walking up and both went inside the house. When they walked in, two boys came out of the kitchen and dapped Quinton up. The two had started working for Read not too long ago and were working their way up. They had just came in to get several dime bags of weed and kilos of cocaine to sell. Read gave them a certain amount that they had to sell by the end of the week to prove themselves.

*"Ya'll be careful out there. Police right down the block."* Quinton told them.

The two boys shook their heads and walked out.

*"Where everybody at man? Tierra told me some shit went down and Read wanted me to come through."* Quinton said to Lil G. He noticed that Lil G got real serious.

*"Man, this boy tried it with Read and Read damn near killed him in the living room. We pulled him off him and made him leave cause he was making a lot of noise, screaming like a little bitch and everything. So I told the boys to call you. Tierra was over here getting money from the girls to give to you and she said she would tell you."* He said.

Quinton thought about when she came to the crib earlier. She didn't mention anything about money she was supposed to be giving me, he thought to himself. He shrugged it off and went back to the conversation.

*"Okay so where is he now?"* he asked.

*"Man, this dude was talking about riding to his girls crib to get at him."* Lil G said.

Quinton pulled his cell phone out to call his boy. Read answered on the first ring.

*"Meet me at the train station now."* He instructed Quinton.

*"Coolin."* Quinton said.

Quinton put his phone back in his pocket and looked at Lil G. *"Let's go."* Lil G put his .45 in his pants and headed off with Quinton.

*"Aye yo, lock up. Put Jaydee on the door."* Quinton told one of the boys that was sitting in the living room.

*"Aight. YoJaydee, door!"* the boy yelled.

Quinton and Lil G hopped in his car and sped over to the

train station. When they pulled up, they searched the lot for Reads car. Quinton looked towards the dumpsters near the back and spotted his 2012 black on black Lexus IS. He pulled into a spot near it, and he and Lil G got out. Read got out the car and looked pissed. Quinton rarely saw Read upset but that day, Read looked like he could spit fire. Quinton was already upset just at the situation. Read was like the big brother that he never had so when someone messed with Read, they messed with him. Read walked over to Quinton's car.

*"Waddup? G tell you what happen?"* Read asked.

*"Yea."* Quinton said. *"Where he at? We can take care of this fuck ass nigga."*

*"He's in the trunk."* Read said. *"He went straight to his bitch house like I thought he would. That nigga tried to get tough and shit in front of her but got knocked the fuck out with my fucking burner."*

Quinton's eyebrows shot up when he heard Read tell him that he was in the trunk of his car. He looked at Lil G who didn't show any type of emotion.

*"Aight so what you wanna do?"* Quinton asked.

*"Take him to the graveyard."* Read said.

*"Aight lets go."* Lil G said.

The graveyard was an old abandoned house in Decatur that Read used to torture the few stupid people that tried him. It was rare that they used the house but when they did, it wasn't for play. Quinton hopped in the car with Read and Lil G and they rode out. Quinton could hear the boy in the trunk making muffled screams.

*"Aye bruh what happened to the chic?"* Quinton asked. *"Didn't you say he ran to his chic's house?"*

*"Yea. She tried to buck up, but the minute that nigga screamed she fell back."* He said laughing.

*"Okay so what you wanna do about her?"* Lil G asked.

*"Oh trust she ain't talking. She a little tied up right now."* Read answered.

Quinton and Lil G left it alone as they continued to drive to the graveyard.

*"Wait hold up. Tierra said she saw two of them. What happened with the other one?"* Quinton asked.

Lil G and Read started laughing hard. Lil G spoke first.

*"Man that was Devonte. He worked for Read before. Read had him with this sucka ass nigga to see if he was straight or not. So when the shit came up short, Devonte let us know."* He said.

*"Oh damn that's wassup."* Quinton said laughing.

*"Yea man. That shit was too funny when Devonte and this dumb ass was standing there and when I asked him about why his money was always coming up short and that nigga started coming up with all these fucking excuses and shit. Then Devonte pulled called that nigga out and ole boy really tried to fucking swing on this nigga. Yo I give that nigga cool points for bravery but, this nigga bout to learn."* Read said.

Quinton shook his head in agreement. *"I feel you man."*

They continued to ride for a few more minutes and pulled up

95

to the deserted house. There was one other car that was there, which let Quinton know that there was someone there awaiting their arrival. Read stopped the car and popped the trunk. Quinton and Lil G walked around to see the boy tied up in the trunk with his right eye swollen and dried up blood around his nose. Reads boy Ahmad came out of the house to help them.

Ahmad had been working for Read for the last few years and always known for brutal punishment. He was his traveling partner and security whenever Read met up with a buyer or seller outside of the state of Georgia. He came down the steps and helped them get the boy out of the trunk. They carried him in the house and into one of the empty rooms. The good thing about the house is that it sat on acres of land, where there were no houses around for miles so, no matter how much anyone screamed, it would be hard for help to arrive. Read said he wanted something that was out of a horror movie and that's exactly what he had in this house.

When they got to the room and dropped the bow, Ahmad grabbed the boy and sat him in the single chair that sat in the middle of the room. The boy tried to kick but when he saw Ahmad put his hand on the handle of his gun, he became still. Together they tied the boy to the chair and ripped the tape off his lips. The boy let out a scream from the pain. Read walked into the room with what appeared to be a large ball of plastic in his hands. He pulled it apart to show that they were plastic ponchos and each one grabbed one. They put the ponchos on and Read stood and watched looking the boy in the eye.

*"So Ricky, what's good my nigga? You was popping all that shit earlier and had the nerve to try me? So you thought you could steal from me and get away with it?"* he asked him calmly.

The boy didn't say a word. Quinton walked up and punched him in his face. The boy groaned in pain still not saying anything.

*"What's the matter Ricky? Cat got your tongue? Aye PK, hit that nigga again. Knock his jaw loose so then maybe he can speak."* Read spat. Quinton did just that. He hit the boy so hard in his jaw, he was sure he broke it. The boy groaned and dropped his head in agony. Still he did not say anything. Quinton could tell that Read was starting to get pissed off at the situation. He was known for

making niggas talk, so for this boy to be sitting there taking the licks and not saying anything, he couldn't have it. He had to fix it, then and there. He worked hard to build his empire and he would be damned if he let some little kid fuck his stuff up.

Read walked over to Ricky and grabbed him by his throat. *"You can cut the bullshit. Ain't nobody harder than me nigga. I told you, I got one rule, never bite the hand that feeds you."* He held out his hand for Yusef to hand him his burner. He put the silencer on and held the gun to his temple at point range. *"Don't worry. I'll tell your bitch you said goodbye."*

Ricky's face frowned in anger. *"Fuck you!"* he spat. Read shot him in the head before he could get the word out.

Ahmad immediately began cleaning up the area and picking up the plastic that was on the floor to trash and burn. Read put his burner away and walked out of the room. *"Let me know when you finish with clean up. PK, Lil G, let's go handle this bitch."* He demanded. They all walked to his car and left to go finish the job.

*

Quinton and Read were driving in the car headed to the strip club. They decided to go blow money at Magic City and get drunk just because. They had just left Ricky's girlfriends house and Read pistol whipped her and left her bleeding in the closet with her pulse slowly fading. He didn't want to kill her but, he wasn't going to jail because her man messed with his money.

*"Man dawg, I don't know about you, but I'm ready to get fucked up. Bout to make these niggas hate on the king tonight!"* Read said as he took a hit of the blunt. He passed the blunt to Quinton and he took a drag of it.

*"Hell yea bruh. You know I'm with it. All this shit that we dealt with today, a nigga deserves some royal treatment. And you know these hoes will do anything for the paper."* Quinton said laughing.

*"Aye my nigga speaking of paper, I need you to take a trip with me."* Read said serious. *"I got to go holla at this nigga in Costa Rica about this new product that can make us some serious money in these streets bruh."*

99

Quinton shook his head as he listened to what Read had to say. Read usually had Ahmad travel with him and he handled the in house stuff while he was away but, he told Read he wanted to get deeper in and this was perfect. *"Aight. Cool with me. Just say when."* He said.

*"Next week."* Read instructed. *"These niggas are heavy hitter'sdawg. You can't come in this shit looking like no tourist. You my nigga and shit but, money is money. Ya feel me?"* he asked him.

*"Hell yea."* Quinton said. *"Now let's get it."*

The two dapped each other up and finished their blunt. They walked inside of Magic City and almost instantly, some of the baddest girls in Atlanta approached them showing them much love. Read walked over to the bar and got $5000 in ones laughing as some of the girls eyes grew large from the potential opportunity to make rent. The two sat down at a table towards the back and the girls ran to the room to get ready to show their skills on the stage. As soon as he sat down, Quinton was approached.

*"Wassup sexy?"* she asked as she pulled up a seat next to him.

*"Wassup slim?"* he asked nonchalant.

*"Hmmm.....you. I done seen you in here a few times before. What's your name?"* she said.

*"They call me Q shawty. What about you?"* he asked not really caring.

*"Princess."* She said sweetly.

Quinton laughed cockily. *"How original."* He said. *"I bet that's your real name too right?"*

*"No. My real name is April. But I go by Princess because that's what I'm treated like once you get these goodies."* She said confident.

Quinton just shook his head as he watched the dancers on the stage. Read looked in amusement.

*"Aye sweetheart, why don't you take my mans in the back and give him the royal treatment then?"* he asked sarcastically.

Quinton turned looking towards Read laughing heartily at Princess ignorance. He saw a look of confusion on her face as she tried to figure out what he meant.

*"Oh you wanna dance?"* she asked standing up grabbing Quinton by the hand. *"Well come on. I got you."* She said.

*"Nah."* Read said. *"If you all that good, why don't you give a taste of the goodies?"*

Realizing what he meant she frowned. *"Oh I don't do that."* She said. "I *got a man.*"

Quinton and Read both laughed. *"Shawty what the fuck your man gotta do with me?!"* Read said as he flashed a stack of hundreds. *"Money talks, bullshit walks. Now what you gone do?"*

Princess grabbed his hand taking him to the back and eager to make the hundreds of dollars Read promised her. She paid the bouncer a couple of hundred bucks to keep his mouth shut. What's a couple of hundred dollars when she could make thousands? Once the curtain closed, she sat him down on the couch and went to work. She knew how to do moves to where if someone was watching the cameras in the champagne room, she was able to make it appear as if she was dancing and not really fucking. She did

102

have a boyfriend like she said. But he was a two bit hustler. She needed someone like Quinton or Read on her arm to pump her up and get her out the club. She decided to give him everything she had to keep him coming back for more.

She slowly twisted and turned her body in his face while brushing against his manhood and grinding on him. She could feel his dick getting hard and showed him her sexy smile. She climbed on top of him dancing and pulling his dick out of his pants. She saw him gliding a condom on his massive hard dick and knew he was with it. She moaned softly in his ear while she eased herself on top of him. She rode him slow making it appear as if she was giving a dance. She allowed him to touch her body and squeeze her as she began to get excited from the feeling.

Quinton wouldn't let on but, he was enjoying everything that she was giving him. He could tell that she knew how to please her man. The way that she bounced up and down on him made his entire body pulsate. He put his hands around her waist and guided her up and down. He wanted to bend her over and pound her ass down but, they were in the champagne room.

All of a sudden the music grew louder in the club and he could tell that money was being thrown at the stage. *No doubt its Read,* Quinton thought to himself.

*Go on shake your ass girl, Im'a throw this money,*

*Go on shake your ass girl, Im'a throw this money,*

*Go on shake your ass girl, Im'a throw this money,*

*Im'a throw this money, Im'a throw this money.*

He knew whoever was on stage was killing it cause that was one of he and Read's money songs. With the music louder, it gave Quinton opportunity to do what he wanted with Princess. Placing his hand over her mouth to keep her from screaming out, he bent her over a small end table that sat in the room. She immediately grabbed her ankles as he dug her insides out. She moaned as she felt every inch of him touching her walls. He could feel himself about to come so he pulled out of her making her turn around to swallow his seed. She tried to back away at first but he grabbed the back of her head and shoved himself into her mouth releasing his loud. She swallowed it all as he fixed himself to go back to the floor.

*"So I'm gonna give you my number for you to call me."* She told him as she took his cell phone he had just pulled out his pockets. She programmed her number in his phone.

Quinton pulled out several hundreds that he had in his roll and gave them to her. *"Aight. I'll think about it."* He told her. He walked out of the room to find his friend throwing several hundreds of dollar bills to the girls on stage at a time as he danced to the music with ass clapping in his face. He walked up next to him and joined in.

*"It's a soldier's life!"* they both yelled as they threw money and drank the night away.

*

## Chapter Four

Tanya sat in living room of her 3 bedroom home that Bishop had bought for her when Quinton was a child. She got up and walked over to the mini bar and poured herself a Jack Daniels Honey with ice. She sat down in her favorite chair and sipped her drink as she cut her television on to drown out the silence. She flipped through the channels and settled on reruns of The Game on BET. She watched the screen aimlessly and felt the tears threatening to escape from her eyes. She blinked them away and took another sip of her drink. Her eyes happened to fall on a picture of Quinton when at his tenth birthday party standing between her and Bishop.

She walked over to the picture picking it up and let the tears fall. It was hard for her accepting the fact that Quinton was now following in his father's footsteps. When Quinton called her six months ago to tell her that he had left his father's house, her heart dropped. She begged him to go back to his father's house or at least come stay with her and he refused saying that he needed his own space. She had heard rumors about him hanging around Bishops old running buddy Read. She knew what he was doing but, she didn't want to believe it.

Tanya couldn't believe how much things have changed since she had Quinton. She wanted nothing but the best for her son to the point that she became Bishops play thing again after confronting him with their son. They messed around for a few months and then Anna tried to kill herself and Bishop let her go. But, he kept his word and continued to be there for their son. It hurt her at first as he grew up because she couldn't teach him certain things his father could but, she saw him whenever she wanted and knew that he was in a good home. Ever since Bishop gave his life to God, she saw such a great change in him and in all honesty, it turned her on even more. She still loved Bishop more than she wanted to admit, but she couldn't act on it because she knew he loved Anna. She didn't want to do anything to jeopardize Bishop helping her, especially now that Quinton was 18. Tanya was in school studying to be a therapist before she got pregnant with Quinton. After she had him, Bishop convinced her to go back to school and even paid her way. Now, she had her own practice as a sex therapist and had a nice life for herself. But she was still lonely.

Tanya picked up the phone to call Bishop. She really hoped that he answered so that she wouldn't have to deal with Anna. Although they were cordial with each other for the sake of the children, they still had negative emotions towards each other from the past. The phone rang twice before she got an answer.

*"White residence."* Traniece answered.

*"Hey Niecey how you doing? This is Tanya."* She said.

*"Hi Miss Tanya. I'm good. You wanna speak to daddy?"* she asked her nicely.

*"Yes baby I need to talk to him about Quinton. Have you heard from him?"* she asked hopefully.

*"No ma'am not since last week."* Traniece answered honestly. *"He came by and took me to get some lunch and hang out but, daddy*

*made me come home cause he didn't want me to hang around him, so if it's not at school, I really don't get to see him, unless he's dropping stuff off to me and even then daddy makes me give it back."* She said with sadness in her voice.

*"I know you miss your brother baby."* Tanya said. *"I know it's hard. Right now, he's just mad at the world. I just really want him to get it together before it's too late. Don't worry baby. It'll be ok."* She told her over the phone.

*"Yes ma'am."* Traniece answered. *"Let me go get daddy for you."*

Tanya heard Traniece put the phone down and walk off to get Bishop. *"Its Miss Tanya."* She heard her say. Bishop picked up the phone. *"Hello Tanya."* He said.

*"Hey Bishop. How are you?"* she asked softly.

*"I'm ok. Preparing to go to the hospital. Sister Beece is in the hospital and the family doesn't think that she will make it."* He told her.

Tanya let out a sigh. *"Well I won't take up too much of your time. I was just trying to find out if you had talked to Quinton."* She asked.

*"No."* he answered shortly.

Tanya was getting frustrated. *"Bishop I know that you don't want to have anything to do with that lifestyle anymore, but that is your son, our son out there! He needs you whether you think he does or not. I can't tell you what to do but, you can't just ignore the problem. You two are so much alike that it's ridiculous. He's my son too Bishop. I don't want him out there selling drugs! What if he gets shot? What if he gets killed? What are you gonna say then huh? You have to help him Bishop. You have to!"* Tanya sobbed.

She could hear Bishop sighing on the phone in frustration.

*"Tanya what do you want me to do? He won't listen to me. He's hard headed and wants to do what he wants to do. He's grown and made his choice."* He said to her.

*"How can you be such a hypocrite?"* Tanya spat.

*"Excuse me?"* he asked.

*"Yes. You heard me; A hypocrite. How can you preach in the*

*pulpit every week and have people turning their lives over to God and asking them to get their lives right when you won't even help your own son? It's like you don't even want to try to save him. What? You're so worried about your image and what everyone else thinks that you aren't even thinking about your son. Or do you only care about one child more than the other?"* she asked as she continued to cry.

She had walked over to pick up the bottle of Jack Daniels and began to drink from the bottle. Bishop could tell that she was upset and he wanted to yell at her but, he let it slide.

*"That's not fair Tanya. You know I love both of my children EQUALLY. I do not choose one over the other and I treat them both the same. But Tanya I'm not going to keep begging him to do right. A man has to learn by his mistakes. That's just life. I pray for him every day and night. There is not a day that goes by that I am not thinking about him or wondering if he's safe. But in his eyes right now, I'm the enemy. He has to be able to come to his own senses at his own time."* He explained.

Tanya let the tears fall as she listened. She knew that Bishop had a point but, she just wanted her son back. He was all that mattered to her.

*"Are you okay?"* she heard him ask.

*"I will be I guess."* She said. *"It just hurts because I want my baby back."* She said as she sniffed.

*"I know. I do too."* He said. *"Just pray. That's what I've learned the hard way. This family has been through a lot and prayer has always got me through. It's going \to get better. Are you going to be ok?"* he asked her.

*"Yea. I guess. I'm home and just gonna go to bed."* She told him.

*"Tanya are you drinking?"* Bishop asked her dryly.

Tanya then sighed. *"Yes. But so what? It's just a few drinks in the safety of my own home. My son is somewhere out in the streets doing God knows what, and I just want to have a few drinks to relax."*

*"Tanya I thought you stopped drinking. You said that you weren't going to be drinking anymore since you started practicing."* He asked

her.

*"I don't drink like that. Just every now and then. Quit nagging me. I'm not your child."* She said with her words slurred.

*"Then stop acting like one."* He mumbled.

*"What? Fuck you Bishop!"* she said as she slammed the phone down. She threw her phone across the room in frustration and watched it break into pieces.

*

Bishop hung up the phone upset at the conversation that he just had with Tanya. They didn't talk as much unless it involved Quinton, but he always had a soft spot for her and cared about her feelings. He sat at his desk in his study and rubbed the temples of his forehead. He heard a knock at his study door and turned to see Traniece standing there.

*"Daddy are you okay?"* she asked him.

*"Yea baby."* He sighed. *"I was just talking to Miss Tanya, and well stuff didn't go so good. But don't worry, I'm okay."*

*"Was it about Quinton?"* she asked quietly.

*"Yea."* He said. *"She was just a little upset at your brother's actions and didn't like my response to it."*

*"Daddy, can I ask you something without getting mad?"* she asked him fidgeting at the door.

Bishop took his glasses off and looked at the serious look on his daughters face. *"Of course. Come on in and sit down. You know you can ask me anything."* He told her.

Traniece came in and sat down in the chair that was opposite her father.

*"Daddy, do you miss Quinton?"* she asked him seriously.

Bishop looked at his daughter puzzled.

*"What would make you ask that?"* he asked her.

*"Well, it just seems like you don't really miss him. I mean I know he's doing some bad stuff right now but, it just seems like you don't care about him. I know it's not polite to eavesdrop but I heard*

*you talking to Miss Tanya just now and you said some really mean things daddy. How do you think mom would feel if that were me that was out there going against you? Would you just write me off too?"* she asked with tears forming in her eyes.

Bishop got up out of his seat and went to Traniece hugging her tightly. *"Of course not baby. I would never want you to think that. I love Quinton. He's my son. Some things, I know it may be difficult for you to understand baby girl. And I was actually about to call Tanya to apologize because I know it's hurting her especially since she's alone."* He told her.

*"I think that's a good idea. I know her and mom aren't friends but I like Miss Tanya. She's always really nice to me and gives me really good advice."* She said smiling.

*"Really?"* Bishop asked surprised.

*"Yea. When Quinton first left she would call here to see if we heard from him and sometimes I would be crying and she would tell me to think about how me and him were close and pray for those times again. Then she would let me vent until I felt better."* She said

as she wiped her eyes with tissue.

Bishop sat back down in his chair and thought about what his daughter just told him. *I didn't know she talked to her like that*, he thought. *I better call her back. I can't believe I went there.*

*"Well daddy, I'm gonna leave you alone. I have to go do my homework. School's almost over so they are giving us a ton of homework and exams."* She got up and kissed her daddy on the cheek before walking to the door. *"You know daddy, Quinton's going to be graduating next week."* She said.

*"Yes I know Traniece. Although I am out of that life, I still keep my ears open."* He told her. *"What are you aiming at?"*

*"Well, maybe we should all go to his graduation. And by all, I mean you too."* She said sweetly.

*"And how do you know he will be there Niecey?"* he asked her.

*"Cause I believe daddy. Cause I believe."* She walked out the room and went upstairs.

Bishop watched as his daughter walked away and smiled. Little did she know, but she just taught him a major lesson. He picked up his phone and tried to call Tanya but it continued to go straight to voicemail. Feeling the guilt, he grabbed his car keys and headed to the garage to head to see Sister Beece at the hospital. I'll try her again on the way, Bishop thought to himself.

Bishop opened the car door to his Cadillac Escalade and climbed in as he opened his garage door. He cut the truck on and backed out of the garage heading towards the hospital. As he drove towards the highway, he tried to call Tanya again in hopes that she would answer.

"*Greetings. You have reached the personal voice mail box of Dr. Tanya Price. I can't get to my phone right now so if you would please leave your name, number, and a brief message, and I will get back to you at my earliest convenience. Thank you and have a great day.*"

Bishop frowned. "*She must have cut her phone off.*" He said out loud. He pulled up to a stoplight and waited on it to turn green. He turned on the ramp to get on Interstate 20 and headed towards

Grady Memorial Hospital. During the fifteen minute drive, he

thought about everything that had happened in the last six months.

He missed his son Quinton more than he could stand. Ever since

Quinton left the house that night, Bishop had tried to throw

himself into his ministry so that he wouldn't think about the pain

he held in his heart. He felt himself drifting away from certain areas

in his life and knew that he had to find balance again. Things were

tense at home between him and Anna because ever since Quinton

left, Bishop was hardly home and when he was, he was always in his

study. He stayed away from Anna because he didn't want to take

his frustrations out on her. He knew she wouldn't understand.

Bishop pulled up to the hospital and parked in the visitors

parking. He tried to call Tanya's phone again before he went inside

the hospital. Again it went straight to voicemail. Saying a quick

prayer, Bishop got out the car and headed towards the entrance of

the hospital heading towards the hospice section of the hospital. He

walked down the halls of the hospital and looked at his cell phone

to see if Tanya had called. He knew that he shouldn't be so pressed

to talk to her but he couldn't help it. He still cared for her well being. After all she was the mother of his oldest child. He had Anna and Traniece and she had no one. He approached the room where Miss Beece rested and gathered himself before walking into her room.

He walked in to find Miss Beece laying in the bed with her son and granddaughter watching television. That's where I know her from, Bishop thought to himself. Miss Beece's granddaughter had attended the church and she caught his attention a few times. He had thoughts of her at times, why he didn't know, but here she was staring him face to face.

*"Well hello there young lady."* Bishop said to break the awkward silence.

*"Hello Bishop!"* Miss Beece said as a smile formed on her face. *"I'm so glad you came."* She said.

*"Of course. You know I have to come and make sure that you are in here behaving yourself. You have to get better lady so that I can see you in the 3rd row pew Sunday."* He said. They both knew that the likelihood of her being released from the hospital was slim.

Miss Beece had been diagnosed with cancer and had decided against treatment so her days were numbered. She told the doctors that she didn't want to send her days taking treatments that although were intended to help her body, would cause severe pain.

*"If the Lord intends for me to stay on His earth, then He will make a way."* She would tell her doctors, family and friends.

Miss Beece smiled at Bishops words and said *"Well Bishop, as much as I would like for that to happen, I think its time or me to go home. My soul is a little tired."*

A hush fell over the room and everyone looked sad at her words. She spoke up quickly. *"Bishop I do apologize. I failed to introduce you to my family. This is my son Melvin Thomas. He came here to visit for a while from Tennessee. And this here is my granddaughter, Alexis. Alexis is here in grad school over at Clark Atlanta. You've seen her before at church with me. She's Melvin's daughter."* She said proudly.

Bishop shook hands with both of them. *"It's nice to meet you. I'm sorry that we had to meet under these circumstances.Mr.*

*Thomas, you should know that your mother is a wonderful part of our church. She was there before I became a pastor and was just a knucklehead."* He said with a light laugh.

Mr. Thomas shook his head and smiled as well.

*"Miss Beece here has a way of getting people to listen to her. That's the kind of leadership we needed at the church. She's part of the reason why I became a pastor. I used to be in the streets and she told me to get my life together. Of course I shrugged it off but, your mother, this wonderful woman, wouldn't give up on me. Now I'm walking Gods path thanks to her."* He took her hand and squeezed it.

Miss Beece smiled and wiped a tear. *"That's because I knew what God had in store for you son. You've had a rough past and your rough days aren't behind you. Now I don't say much on it but, I know what's going on between you and Quinton. Now I don't know the whole story but that boy doesn't belong in them streets. Now I know you love your son. You got to save him and show him the way to God."*

Bishop not wanting to be disrespectful listened to what she had to say. *"Yes ma'am. I am praying for him to come home every day. Now I don't want you to be worrying about that right now Miss Beece. I want you to just relax and take care of yourself."*

Miss Beece wasn't stopping. *"I'm good and relaxed son so no need to worry about that. You got to do more than pray to save your son. You got to go and get him Bishop. You know coming from them streets what they can do to that boy. Don't let him go down that path. There is still time. Now if you really want me to get better, you go and bring that boy home. That will make me better."* She said in a stern voice.

*"Yes ma'am."* He said. He looked over at Mr. Thomas who was giving an apologetic look.

*"Now you see what I went through as a kid."* Mr. Thomas said with a laugh. *"She is not just going to let something go."*

*"That's my nana."* Alexis said with a smile as she kissed her grandmother on the cheek.

*"That's right baby. Now nana is getting tired. I think I need to rest for*

*a little bit."* Miss Beece said.

*"Ok Miss Beece, I'm going to go ahead and let you get your rest. I will come and see you tomorrow okay?"* Bishop asked her.

*"That's alright son. You just remember what I said."* She told him.

Bishop, Melvin, and Alexis walked out the room as Miss Beece settled to go to sleep. When they reached the hallway, Melvin laughed a little more.

*"Sorry about that in there. When my momma gets on something, it's hard to get her to let it go."* Melvin said.

Bishop shook his head in laughter. *"I understand brother. Its ok. I see her every Sunday in the church fussing at a few members so I know."*

*"Yea when I came here to go to school, she told me the first day that I needed to find a church home."* Alexis said.

*"Well I'm glad that you chose Pearly Gates. If you ever need anything, my doors are always open."* Bishop told her.

*"Thank you Bishop. I appreciate that. We look forward to seeing you Sunday and please continue to keep my grandmother in your prayers."* She asked solemnly.

*"Of course."* Bishop pulled out his card and handed one to both her and her father. *"My number is on that card. Please don't hesitate to call. Good evening."* He said as he walked back towards his car.

*

Tanya awoke to a knocking at her door. She had fallen asleep on the couch next to the empty bottle of Jack Daniels that she had drank earlier when she talked to Bishop on the phone. She heard the tapping again at her door and got up to see who it was. Her head was spinning from the amount of alcohol that was consumed as she made her way across the living room floor. She walked over to the door, looking out the peep hole and saw Bishop standing there. She opened the door frustrated.

*"What are you doing here? Its late."* She said as he walked into her apartment.

*"Well hello to you too. And it's not late. Its only 9pm. I called you several times. Why didn't you answer the phone?"* Bishop asked her observing everything in the living room. He saw the empty liquor bottle on the floor and shook his head. *"I guess I have the answer. The entire bottle Tanya?"* he asked.

Tanya walked past him and sat down on the chair. *"I broke my phone earlier after I talked to you so I couldn't answer my phone okay? And yes I drank the bottle. One of us has to mourn our son. It seems like I'm the only one that cares about him."* She said with tears in her eyes.

*"Tanya stop it! Now you are not going to keep placing the blame on me as to our son. I want him home. I do. But I also know that he is not going to come willingly. It doesn't help when you are blaming me all the time."* He said loudly.

*"I'm not blaming you."* Tanya said crying. *"All I'm asking you to do is save our son. Get him off the streets and bring him home. I'm not asking you to turn him into a Bible thumper but, at least acknowledge he exists. You act like he never existed at all."* Tanya got

up and walked over to her mini bar looking for something to drink.

Bishop walked over to her snatching the bottle that she picked up out of her hand. *"Give me this!"* he said as she stumbled.

Tanya reached for the bottle but Bishop was quick in getting it out of arms reach. *"Stop trying to control me. I'm not your little side chic anymore to where I do whatever you say. You have a wife that does that remember?"* she asked sarcastically.

Bishop took the bottle sitting it down and grabbing Tanya tightly shaking her to get her attention. *"Stop it Tanya! Do you hear me? Just stop it. Look at what you are doing to yourself."* He said as he held her by her arms. Tanya looked up at him with so much hurt in her eyes. She cried out letting out all of her vulnerabilities and Bishops heart softened. He pulled her close to him letting her cry into his chest. Tanya sobbed and sobbed repeatedly saying *"I want my baby back."*

Bishop held her tight letting her get it all out of her system. Tanya looked up at him and said, *"I miss him so much Bishop. I just want my baby home."*

Bishop looked down at her seeing her look so pitiful and holding her, placed his lips on hers softly. The two began to kiss passionately and embraced each other. Moments later, Bishop broke away realizing what was done, as the two pulled apart still panting.

*"This isn't right."* Bishop stated. *"I'm married and you're drunk. I shouldn't have done that. I'm so sorry. I didn't mean for it to happen."* He said.

Tanya pushed him away in frustration. *"You never do Bishop. You always play with my emotions, and then throw her in my face!"* she yelled in a drunken slur. *"You keep popping up and telling me you care about my wellbeing and all this bullshit."* She started throwing pillows and everything she could get her hands on at him.

Bishop grabbed her and pushed her against the wall to keep her from throwing anything else. *"Tanya stop! Just stop okay? You're drunk and don't know what you are saying. I'm sorry. I wasn't trying to upset you. I know this is hard for you."* He let her go and she walked around the living room hysterically.

*"You know Bishop I swear that's all I hear from you is I'm sorry. You were sorry when you started messing with me eighteen years ago and told me you loved me. You were sorry when you got me pregnant and made me keep my baby a secret so you could protect your relationship. I never came at you like most of these bitches would! I was 16 and by myself because of you. Now you sorry? Were you sorry when you threw your perfect little family in my face? No. You don't think I know that Quinton told me about how Anna treats him? Yea. Little Miss First Lady making my baby feel unwelcomed in his own home because he came from me! You're always sorry Bishop! That shit is getting old. You can keep your apologies. Cause I have enough from you to last a lifetime."* Tanya walked off to her room leaving Bishop standing looking shocked.

Bishop stood in Tanya's living room taking in everything that she had just told him. He knew that she still had a lot of emotions built up as to how she felt towards the situation he put them in but he never thought she still had feelings towards him. *What am I going to do?* He thought to himself. He didn't know if he should leave, or if he should go talk to her. Choosing to do the latter, he walked to her closed bedroom door and knocked.

*"Go home to your family Bishop."* She said through her closed door. *"Just let me pine over my son in peace."*

Bishop opened her bedroom door and stepped in to see her laying on her bed with her pillow stained with fresh tears. *"So you don't think I miss our son? Huh? You don't think that I don't know what he's out there doing and worry that he could get killed? I've been there. You of all people know this. I want him home T. I do."* He said with exasperation.

Tanya sat up and looked at Bishop in his eyes. *"Then what is stopping you from bringing him home huh? What?"* she pleaded.

*"Honestly, I don't know how. I always know what to do or say when it comes to everything; Church, work, whatever. But when I left the streets, it was for my own reasons. I don't know if Quinton can leave and be safe. I feel like I failed him as a father. From the day I found out about him, a lot of wrongs were done. I failed as a father."* He felt the tears begin to fall from his face and couldn't stop them.

Tanya wasn't sure how to react at what she was seeing. Bishop broke down and let the tears flow. He really missed his son and wanted him home. He knew that Quinton was in dangerous territory. Tanya leaned over and grabbed his hand. She gave it a squeeze as she hugged him allowing him to cry on her shoulder. Bishop looked at her through tear stained eyes. He was trying to fight the urges that he was having but it was something in Tanya's eyes that made him want to be with her at that moment.

He cupped her chin in his hand and kissed her slowly and passionately. Tanya was taken back and asked in between his kisses *"Bishop what are you doing? You said you couldn't do this."* He silenced her by placing his lips on hers and exploring her mouth with his tongue. She moaned and gave in allowing his mouth to explore hers. She placed her hand on the back of his head and caressed it as they continued to kiss passionately. Bishop took his hands and began to rub and caress her body exploring the very curves that he fell for in the first place. He aid her on the bed and began to kiss her body from  head to toe as she began to cry out. When he got to her thighs he felt her take a sharp breath and slowly began to make his way to her pearl to taste her sweetness.

She cried out as his tongue caressed every crevice and tears fell down her face.

Bishop placed his body over hers and she put her hands on his back caressing him as he entered her slowly. Tanya was so caught up in everything that she didn't think about the fact that he had a wife. All she cared about at that moment was that he was hers. He stroked her slowly and gently, both enjoying the feeling that they were giving each other. The two consoled each other making love until the wee hours of the morning.

*

Bishop woke up realizing that he had fallen asleep in Tanya's bed. He sat up and looked down at her resting peacefully as he thought back to what had happened a few hours before. *Oh God, what have I done?* He thought to himself. He sat in the bed a few moments collecting himself and thinking about the mistake that he just made. He knew that it was wrong when he was in the middle of doing the act. He should have stopped but it was the wrong time to hurt her again. He didn't want to think of it as pity sex but, he knew that if he had stopped, things wouldn't have ended well.

He slowly got out of the bed so as to not wake her and began looking for his clothes. He remembered tossing them to the dresser in the corner when they were in their moment of passion. He picked up his clothes and headed to the bathroom to get dressed. He closed the bathroom door quietly and turned on the light and saw his reflection in the mirror. Holding his head down he knew he was in a world of trouble. *How am I going to explain this to Anna?* He thought. *She is going to kill me. Its 3 in the morning,* he thought as he looked at his watch. He quickly cleaned himself up, got dressed and exited the bathroom.

He crept towards the bedroom door when he heard Tanya's voice.

*"You're leaving?"* she asked in a groggy tone. *"Are you sure that you don't want to stay?"*

He looked at her and sighed. *"Now you know the answer to that Tanya. It wouldn't be a good idea for either of us."*

Tanya sat up in her bed pulling the covers up to shield herself.

*"I know. I just thought that, well with what just happened, that maybe you had changed your mind."*

Bishop paused at the bedroom door. *"I have to go now. But we will talk later. I'll call you."* He closed her bedroom door and left for her apartment. He got in his car and pulled his cell phone out of the glove box and saw that he had several missed phone calls from Anna and a few text messages.

*9:48pm Anna: Hey call me when you get this.*

*10:32pm Anna: Quinton called.*

*11:15pm Anna: Are you ok?*

*12:21am Anna: Ok its after midnight and you're still not home. What the hell is going on?*

Bishop sighed and cranked his car thinking of what he would tell his wife when he got home. He drove with what seemed to be the weight of the world on his shoulders as he thought about everything that had transpired in the last 12 hours. He couldn't shake the conversation that he had with Miss Beece about Quinton and the mistakes that he made.

*"Father, what am I to do? I feel like I am spiraling out of control."* He said out loud. *"I don't know what I'm doing anymore. I don't know what just happened. I know it was wrong God but, I don't know why but, it just, it just felt like it was supposed to happen. I need you to show me what to do God. I need direction. I need to bring my son home but how? How can I show him the right way without straying from you more than I already have?"* he prayed.

Bishop continued to drive and have his conversation with God. He knew that things were hard right now and he just wanted to make them right. He pulled up to his house and the lights were out. Rather than open the garage to park his truck, he parked on the street and walked up the walkway. He opened the door and the alarm notified him and everyone else in the house that the door was being opened and to disarm the alarm. He quickly disarmed and rearmed the alarm and crept up the steps towards the master bedroom.

He opened the door and quickly began to undress. The bedside light cut on suddenly startling him.

*"Its damn near 4am Bishop!"* Anna yelled at him. *"Where the hell have you been?!"*

Bishop took a deep breath and tried to calmly talk to his wife. *"Anna I'm sorry. I've been running back and forth and I haven't really rested today. After I left from seeing Miss Beece in the hospital, I went to my car and I needed to pray. I ended up falling asleep in the hospital parking lot."* He quickly lied. He was in no way going to tell her that he had slept with his child's mother in the heat of the moment.

*"That's bull Bishop and you know it. You didn't answer your phone. I called you over ten times and sent you several text messages and you didn't respond to anything! You could have been lying dead somewhere. I called everybody looking for you, including Tanya who told me that she talked to you on the phone which you failed to mention. So where were you? Were you with her? Huh? Answer me!"* his wife demanded.

*"Baby, no. I talked to her on the phone because she was upset*

over Quinton. I did talk to her on the phone but that was before I went to the hospital." He thought back quickly to her calling the house earlier and Traniece answering it. "She called the house earlier and I spoke with her briefly before I went to the hospital. I stayed with Miss Beece and counseled her and her family for a while, and I was just exhausted baby. I'm sorry I didn't answer my phone. It was in my glove box in the truck. You know I have a habit of leaving it in there. I apologize for not turning the ringer on. If one of the staff members didn't come to wake me up, I might still be sleep now." He explained to her hoping that she would believe him.

He could see that she was starting to calm down so he came to her side. "I am so sorry Ann. You know I wouldn't do anything to scare you. We have had enough of that already." He kissed her forehead and she sighed.

"Byron I'm just tired of dealing with all of this drama. I'm tired of playing perfect wife like everything is okay in the family its not. Now Tanya is not my best friend by far, and I do feel for her with what she is going through with Quinton being out in the streets but, I don't like this. I love Quinton. God knows I do. But he is weighing our *family down."* She said trying not to get upset.

Bishop looked at her as if she was crazy. *"Anna, what are you trying to say? That's my son. He is a part of our family. Period. I'm not going to outcast him because of the fact that you don't like his mother. What kind of father would I be? How can you even love a man that is a father to one and not the other? I'm not saying that this is easy for any of us. But despite the fact that Quinton is doing wrong right now, he is still my son."* He said sternly.

*"I'm not saying ignore him and outcast him!"* she said getting upset. *"You know what? Nevermind. I'm not dealing with this tonight. Good night."* she yanked the covers over her, turned her back to Bishop, cut the light off and went to sleep.

Bishop sighed and went to the bathroom to prepare for bed. *"God."* He said. *"I need your help. I'm losing control of everything and my family is slipping away from me. Please God, show me what I am to do."* He changed his clothes, got into bed and went to sleep.

*

Bishop and Anna woke a few hours later to Bishops car alarm

going off. Bishop jumped out of his bed and ran downstairs to see what caused it to go off. He went outside and saw that his wind shield had been broken. He walked closer to the car and saw that there was a brick with a note tied around it. He looked around to make sure that he wasn't in any danger and opened the door. He looked up to see Anna looking from the door. He grabbed the note and went back inside to let Anna know that he was ok.

*"What happened?"* she asked him.

*"Someone put a brick through my wind shield."* He said clearly upset and shook.

*"A brick?"* she asked confused. *"Why would somebody do that? Who would do that? Is it something you're not telling me?"* she asked him.

Bishop shook his head and remembered the note attached to the brick. *"You know the same thing that I do. But I bet this will tell us."* He said as he pulled the note off the brick.

*Better get your black suit. Your son's a dead man.*

*"What does it say?"* Anna asked as she saw Bishops entire

demeanor change. Bishop showed her the note and she panicked.

*"Oh my God!"* she said. *"What are we gonna do? What has Quinton done? How did they know how to find us?"* she rolled the questions out.

*"Anna I don't know. Calm down. I will handle this."* Bishop said trying to get his thoughts together.

*"How can I calm down? Somebody threw a brick through your windshield which means that they know where we live."* She said hysterically.

Bishop began pacing back and forth. *"How about someone is trying to kill my son Anna? My son? Does that not matter to you? I know you're worried but, could you at least act like you care about him?"* he asked her highly upset.

*"I just, I don't want anything to happen to anybody. I'm sorry ok? I don't know whats going on. I mean damn Byron, one minute, you're here at the house, and the next thing I know, you are coming home early hours in the morning and then mysteriously, there's a brick in your car."* She said rambling.

Bishop was starting to get pissed off. *"Are you really talking about this again? Seriously? What does one thing have to do with the other? I'm not having this conversation right now."* He stormed up the steps to get his cell phone to call Quinton.

*"Where are you going?"* she asked.

*"To check on my son."* He said as he continued to walk up the steps not looking at her.

*"Byron!"* she said attempting to get his attention.

Bishop stopped and slowly turned towards her. *"What is it Anna?"* he asked.

She hesitated before she responded. *"Just, please be careful. I know that you have a son that you need to think about, but you also have a daughter too. And they BOTH need you safe."* She emphasized. *"So please, don't go anything stupid. You've come too far."* She said with concern.

Bishop stood at the top of the stairwell and absorbed her words. He turned walking towards the bedroom to call his eldest son. God had given him his sign.

*

**Chapter Five**

Read was pulling up to Quinton's apartment so that they could head to the airport. They were going to Costa Rica for a few days to get a new product that Read had been hearing about. He pulled up to call Quinton when his cell phone rang with an unknown number.

*"Hello?"* he answered.

*"Hello Read."* The voice said.

*"Aye man, who this? Son I ain't got time for the games."* Read was about to hang up because this was ten seconds of his life wasted.

*"This is Bishop. Where's Quinton?"* he asked.

Read was in disbelief of what he was hearing. *"Bishop?"* he questioned. *"Ok so, I'm just supposed to believe that all of a sudden after nineteen years that Bishop White is calling my cell phone. Real talk kid, you can cut all that shit.*" He hung up the phone.

Read blew the horn to let Quinton know that he was outside and as he was getting ready to call him to tell him to come outside, his cell phone number rang again.

"*What?*" he responded.

"*Perhaps I didn't make myself clear the first time Read. This is Bishop. Now in case you are worried about authentication of my identity, I know your real name is Markel Wallace, you came and worked for me straight off the bus from New York, you have a son, Junior who is now pretty much the same age as my son, and you THINK, you are the biggest dealer in the game. But realize as easy as it was for me to get your number son, I still have a lot of pull in Atlanta as to how to reach you. Now I'm going to ask you again, where is Quinton?*" Bishop asked aggravated.

Read listened to everything that Bishop said and realized that this wasn't a game and he was actually speaking to the man that got him started in the drug game. "*Man, Bishop, my bad. I didn't know it* was you. I mean dawgits been like almost twenty years. How, how did you get my number?" he asked seriously.

"I told you what I want. Where is my son?" Bishop asked clearly.

Read sighed "Do you really want to hear where he is? Cause from my understanding, you didn't want him around me and even though we hustled together, you told him to stay away. But since you wanna know, we on the way to do a trip. Just like you used to do. And I don't need to hear no sermon from you preacher man."

Bishop laughed into the phone. "Son I assure you, I'm not going to give you a sermon. All I want is my son; alive. So whatever you need to do to get my son back to me, you need to do it." He told him.

"Yo first off, I ain't your son. And second, you gave this shit up to do you. If Q wanna roll with me, he can. I ain't gonna stop him. He a grown ass man. I mean I ain't saying that he under my thumb but, I ain't gonna force nobody. You talk to him yourself." He said trying to figure out why Bishop was calling him after all these years. He could hear Bishop mumbling something under his breath. "Look man, I got work to do. Nice talking to you and all that stuff but, we *got moves to make."*

*"I'm letting you know, Quinton is my blood. And if anything happens to my blood, yours will be all over Bankhead."* Bishop said low and stern.

Read wasn't fazed by what he heard. *"Yea aight. I'm good."* he said.

*"You've been warned."* Bishop said and disconnected the call.

Read sat in his car and looked at his phone. Deep down he was a little nervous because from what he remembered, Bishop was not the person you messed with. His phone rang again and he hesitated before he saw Quinton's name pop up on his caller id.

*"Yo where you at?"* Quinton asked.

Deciding against saying anything then, Read told him he was downstairs. He waited a few minutes in his car for Quinton to come down. He was going to tell Quinton on the plane what happened just in case he needed to prepare himself. Quinton came downstairs and got into the car.

*"Wassupbruh?"* he asked as he closed the door.

*"Whats good son?"* Read said pulling the car out of the parking lot.

*"Ain't nothing bruh. Just tryna get out of here. Tierra asking me a million fucking questions and shit dawg. Her ass getting real fucking clingy and shit. She talking bout some she don't want me going out the country cause she don't know what I'm gonna be doing. I'm like what the fuck, we ain't fucking married or no shit like that. Damn she know what it is."* He said frustrated with her. He felt his phone going off in his pocket and pulled it out to see that Tierra had texted him. *"Damn I ain't even down the street yet and shawty is bugging!"* he said.

Read smirked at Quinton's little love spat. *"What she talking bout?"* he asked.

Quinton opened his phone and read the text out loud.

*"Don't bring me nothing back while you down there fucking them hoes."* He told Read.

*"Yo slim is buggin kid. Where all this shit come from?"* Read

asked now interested.

"*Man, I ran into this chic from school or whatever and I gave her my number on some shit for her brother. All of a sudden, she up on me like we attached or some shit. I'm like dawg, I ain't got time for the clingy shit. So I told her to calm the fuck down and I bounced.*" Quinton said relieved to be getting out of the house.

"*I feel you bruh.*" Read said.

Quinton remembered the money she forgot to mention to him. "*Oh yea, plus, I forgot to tell you the other day when we handled ole boy, shawty didn't tell me she went to the house to collect. Lil G told me he saw her collecting money from the girls. I was thinking she was just over there until I found that out. So I ask shorty whats up with that and she fuckin flip out and shit on some whole, I'm accusing her type shit. Fuckin crazy man.*"

Read immediately went back to the money she had mistakenly not mentioned. "*So did slim give you the money?*" he asked wanting to make sure neither one of them was trying to take his money.

"*Oh yea I got that shit. I told her if you would've found out that she could've gotten her fucking neck snapped. So she know. Trust it ain't gonna happen again."* He told him confidently.

*"Cool. Cool. Tierra good peoples but, I don't play with no nigga when it come to my money."* Read said seriously.

*"I got you bruh."* Quinton told him. *"Money over bitches. Soldiers for life."* He stated to reaffirm his loyalty to him.

Read decided to mention his phone call to Quinton.

*"Hey bruh, have you talked to your pops lately?* He asked him.

Quinton looked at him trying to figure out where the question came from as they continued to drive to the airport. *"Nah man. Why what's good?"* he asked him.

Read hesitated before responding as if trying to find the best way to tell him. *"Your pops called me a few minutes ago when I came to pick you up kid. He was on some weird shit though."*

*"Wait hold up."* Quinton interrupted Read. *"Are you sure it was pops and not some nigga playing around? Like why would he call*

*you? What the fuck for? I ain't spoke to him in months. How you know it was really him?"* Quinton fired questions at him.

*"Son I don't know. But what I do know is he was tryna threaten me saying that if some shit popped off he was coming. That nigga was like 'you been warned'. Like I don't play that shit B. Your pops is a fucking legend but right now, I run these streets you feel me?"* He said angrily. Deep down he was a little concerned but, he didn't need for Quinton to know that.

Meanwhile Quinton's head was reeling with questions. He really hoped his father wasn't trying to get him to come back home because that wasn't going to happen. *"Damn kid. My bad. I'm going to hit him up when we get to the airport."* He told him.

*"Nah man, hit that nigga up now. I don't have time for this ABC drama. He fucking with my time, which is fucking with my money."* He said.

Quinton shook his head in agreement pulling out his cell phone to make the call to his father. He was nervous because he didn't know what his father was going to say but, he had to make sure that he didn't piss Read off before this trip. This was the first serious run that he was doing with Read outside of local trips and he was ready to make some serious money. He dialed the number and listened to the phone ring.

*"Hello?"* Anna answered.

*"Hey its Quinton. Where's pops?"* he asked dryly.

*"Oh my God Quinton! Where are you? Are you okay? Did you have anything to do with Byron's windshield being broken?"* she shot out.

Quinton frowned up. *"Yo what are you talking about? Pops called looking for me. All I wanna know is where he at?"* he was getting agitated with everything that was going on and just wanted answers. He could hear Bishop in the background asking Anna who she was talking to.

*"Just put him on the phone."* Quinton snapped.

*"Hello son."* Bishop greeted Quinton.

*"Yea, wassup? I heard you were looking for me?"* Quinton

asked.

"*Yes, I am. Where are you? I'm assuming with Read?*" Bishop asked tense.

"*Yea. About to roll out to Costa Rica.*" He said then noticing that Read gave him a look of disapproval for telling him where they were going. "*What you need? Is Niecey okay?*" he asked.

"*Yes Quinton your sister is fine.*" Bishop said and began to open up. "*Look son, I know you and I have our differences. I can only tell you from experience that what you are doing now is extremely dangerous and you don't know who or what is out there that can get you. These people that are smiling in your face are around because of what you can do for them. Son, I want you to come home. Come home so that we can work this out and be a family again. Your mother misses you and is torn, your sister misses you, Anna misses you, we all miss you. Just come home.*" He pleaded with him.

Quinton showed no emotion to Read but he felt a small twinge of regret for what he did to his family. It wasn't like he was intentionally trying to hurt them but, he was just wanting to do his own thing. He knew what he was doing was wrong but, he loved it. He loved the thrill of making money. He was smart about his and never put his face out there to avoid getting caught. He missed his family, and he knew he mother was probably in tears but, he wasn't ready to give it up.

*"Look man, I'm good. I ain't walking away like some people."* Quinton said throwing a hint to his father. He heard Bishop sigh in frustration from his comment.

*"Son, I walked away to take care of my family. Nothing is worth me losing my children."* He said.

*"You walked away because your wife shot herself. I told you, I know all about it. Keep it real. She couldn't stand me from jump. I ain't got time for it man, or this conversation. So to answer your question, I'm around and I'm good."* he said.

*"Well then why am I looking at a note that was attached to a brick thrown through my windshield?"* Bishop asked.

Quinton looked at the phone as if he didn't hear what Bishop just said. *"What are you talking about?"*

152

"*Earlier this morning, I was awakened to my alarm going off on the truck and I went and saw that there was a brick thrown through my windshield with the note saying that I needed to prepare or your funeral. So son you're not good when you have someone that is obviously sending a message that your time is limited.*" He explained.

Quinton wasn't fazed by what he heard. "*Ok. Well, I will take care of it. Now I gotta go, anything else?*"

"*Son please. Think about what you are doing. Someone out there wants you dead. That's not something to take lightly. Get out while you can. Walk away now before it's too late.*" He warned.

"*I'm good. Look I gotta go. Tell Niecey I will hit her up when I get back.*" Quinton said before he hung up the phone.

Quinton turned his phone off and threw it in his backpack. "*So, somebody threw a brick in my pops shit and he coming down on me telling him that they are threatening to kill me, talking about I need to walk away and all this shit. I ain't got time for it man.*" He said.

"*Well look man I feel you and everything, and I know your*

pops is worried and shit but, you gotta focus man. I need your head
in the game right now." He said as they pulled into the airport.

"I'm focused man." Quinton said. He was starting to get
pissed off because it seemed like he had to keep explaining himself.

Read looked at him without not saying anything immediately.
He put the car in park and got out walking to the trunk. "Get the
bags." Quinton grabbed the bags out of the trunk and followed
behind him. Read suddenly stopped and turned to Quinton. "I hope
you are as focused as you say man. Because like I said before, money
trumps all." He turned back around and walked toward the doors of
the airport.

Quinton paused at Reads words and reaffirmed that this was
what he wanted, heading to follow his friend to the door to board
the plane to Costa Rica.

*

Bishop sat in his study looking at the phone as Quinton ended
the conversation. He looked around at the room at nothing in
particular and took in what just happened. He let out a sigh and

before he knew it he felt tears stinging his eyes. He knew what he had to do to save his son, but he knew he would be going against God. Bishop got down on his knees and held a picture of Quinton close to his heart.

*"Father,"* he said out loud. *"I'm about to do something that I know is against your will. Quinton is my only son and he's out there in the streets and he needs my help. Lord I know that I am about to do some very wrong things and I ask for your forgiveness in advance. But this is my son and I can't lose him to the streets. I won't lose him. Watch over him Lord. I can't be with him every second of the day. But I gotta do what I gotta do. Keep him and my family under your protection. Forgive me Father."* He said.

Bishop got up and grabbed his cell phone. He dialed a number and a voice answered on the first ring.

*"Speak."* The voice answered.

*"Hey. It's Bishop."* He said low.

*"Bishop? What's good man? It's been a long time man. How you been?"* the voice asked.

*"I'm okay brother. Doing the best that I can. But this ain't a social call. Let me speak to Deuce."* Bishop said.

*"Aight man. Hold on I'll get him for you."* He said and sat the phone down. Bishop could hear him in the background. *"Aye yo Deuce man, phone for you. You ain't gone believe who it is man!"* Deuce picked up the phone.

*"Who this?"* he asked.

*"Deuce. Bishop."* He said.

*"Bishop? Man what's good? I didn't think I would hear from you again. What you need man?"* he asked excited to hear from his old partner.

Deuce was Bishops running partner when Bishop was on the streets hustling. Deuce had all the connects, knew everybody and everything. He was still in the game and many of the dealers in Atlanta came to him for their product. He had his had in everything and the police department on his payroll. Deuce was untouchable.

*"Look man, I never thought I would be going through this*

*again but, my son Quinton, he's in trouble."* Bishop said. *"He's out there selling and I'm getting death threats about him."*

Deuce sat at the other end of the phone shaking his head. *"Yea man, I heard. I know he been going hard now for about six months now with the young nigga Read. I had heard about it a while ago when Read came to cop one day but, I thought you knew about it."* He said.

*"Yea man I knew. He moved out six months ago and it's been hard man."* Bishop told him. *"I don't know how to cope sometimes man. But I gotta save my son."*

*"Yea he's been in a lot of people's conversations lately. It's funny bruh cause in a lot of ways he reminds me of you. He's a hard hitter man. The boy puts in work. He got his hand in a little bit of everything and is in charge of the Soldiers now."* Deuce told him.

Bishop listened to the information that Deuce was giving him to figure out exactly what was going on. *"Any enemies that you know of?"*

*"Nah man, I ain't heard much. The only thing I know of is*

*some lil nigga named Ray Ray. From what I hear, Quinton took his*

*spot as the boss and the lil nigga got embarrassed in front of*

*everybody. From my understanding, he was pissed off at Quinton, but*

*I ain't heard nothing since then."* Deuce informed him.

*"I told Quinton that he had to be careful man."* Bishop said.

*"Why what happened?"* Deuce asked.

Bishop sighed. *"A few days ago Anna and I were at home and*

*someone had thrown a brick through the windshield of my truck.*

*When I went out there to see, it was a note that was wrapped around*

*it saying that somebody was going to kill Quinton and that I*

*basically needed to get ready for his funeral."* He told him.

*"Damn. That's crazy. Too close to home. What did Anna say?*

*How is she by the way? And the baby girl?"* he asked.

*"They're good man. Traniece is almost grown and boy crazy.*

*Anna, well she's still Anna."* Bishop answered with a sigh of

frustration.

Deuce started laughing. *"Let me guess. She still got a little bit of thug in her?"* he asked.

*"Yea man. That morning I came home late and she flipped out. I don't man. I think she still hasn't accepted Quinton even after all these years. I'm trying to keep her happy but man this is my son."* He said.

*"I hear you man. But you gotta remember she been around since day one. Shawty watched you dip out on her a lot."* Deuce said. *"And I told you that she was a little crazy bruh. You know how to pick em."* He said with a laugh.

*"Yea man but, she gotta know my kid comes first. After all these years you would think that she would learn by now."* Bishop said.

*"So what you wanna do bruh?* Deuce asked him seriously.

*"What I gotta do man. I need you to put me back in."* Bishop answered him hoping that he was doing the right thing.

*"But you said you would never go back man. A lot has changed and a lot of these young niggas will try you. He may find out*

*about you. Are you sure about this?"* Deuce asked him.

Bishop thought briefly to what he told him. *"It's my son. Ain't nothing more serious than that. I'm back. Bishop is taking over the streets of Atlanta."* He said with his heart heavy.

*"Aight then bruh. Meet me at the crib tomorrow. We got work to do."* Deuce said.

The two hung up the phone. Bishop took his clerical collar off, hanging it up on his desk. He began to take off his crucifix and thought twice on it. *"I'm going to need this."* He said as he walked upstairs to break the news to his wife.

*

Quinton sat on the plane and looked out the window thinking about the conversation that he had with his father a few hours ago. He had spent majority of the plane ride sleeping and was now wide awake listening to his head phones. He looked across from him and saw that Read was stretched out in the seats asleep. Quinton pulled his laptop out of his carry on and decided to log on to Facebook. He logged on and started checking up on his notifications and messages. He rarely got on Facebook because it was nothing but friend requests from people he didn't really talk to before he started hustling who all of a sudden wanted to get cool with him. He scanned through his messages to see he had gotten a message from Maxine about graduation. He wanted Maxine bad. He read the message to see she wanted a count on who all was participating in Senior Day rituals before graduation.

Quinton was still in school and a few weeks from graduating. He wasn't really into all of the school boy, pep rally things. He just wanted his diploma so he could be out and focus on hustling full time. Read agreed when he said he wanted to get his diploma so that he could prove his father wrong. He decided to send her an instant message to see if she would respond.

*Quinton "Q" White: Whats good lady?*

He scrolled through his timeline and saw some of his classmates posting countdowns and various things about graduation. His message box lit up showing that he had a new message. He went to his inbox and saw that he had a message from someone that he didn't know name Darius.

*Tic tocmuthafucka. Your day is coming.*

Quinton tried to click on the fake name to see who sent the message and what their profile was about, but of course, they had already deactivated the account. *These fuck ass niggas think they can scare me.* Quinton thought to himself. *Bitch ass nigga couldn't even face me like a man.* Quinton deleted the message and got ready to log off Facebook until he heard the familiar ding letting him know that he had an instant message. He looked to see that it was from Maxine.

*Maxine "DivaIAm" Carter: Hey.*

Quinton smiled and began to respond hoping that he could get to know her a little bit more.

*Quinton "Q" White: So what are you up to?*

*Maxine "DivaIAm" Carter: Finalizing some stuff or Senior Day. Are you coming or do you have to "work"?*

Quinton smirked at her sarcasm.

*Quinton "Q" White: I don't know yet. Do I get a chance to see your beautiful face?*

*Maxine: Seriously Quinton? Not tryna be funny but dude you have a girl. A girl that has made it well known that if anyone so much as looks your way that it's trouble.*

Before he could respond, another incoming message came in.

*TierraluvsQ: I thought you and Read were on the plane to Costa Rica? What are you doing on Facebook?*

Quinton rolled his eyes and responded.

*Quinton "Q" White: Yea babe we are still on the plane. They have something called the internet on the airplane. Lol.*

*TierraluvsQ: Shut up. I was just checking.*

Quinton remembered that he was talking to Maxine and messaged her.

*Quinton "Q" White: Shawty I don't belong to nobody. But I could belong to you if you let me.*

*Maxine "DivaIAm" Carter: Goodnite Quinton. I will see you at Senior Day, 9am.*

*Quinton "Q" White: ☺G'nite.*

Quinton smiled as he got ready to log out. He thought briefly to the message that he received from the mysterious person and instant messaged Tierra.

*Quinton "Q" White: Hey have you been getting any weird messages lately?*

*TierraluvsQ: No. Why? One of your groupies stalking you?*

*Quinton "Q" White: Really? Are we back on this shit again? Imtryna make sure shit is good and you wanna beef through fuckin FB?*

Quinton closed the laptop and noticed the sun rising. He pulled the shade down over the window and closed his eyes thinking about what was to come in Costa Rica.

*

*"You did what?!"* Anna screamed at Bishop.

*"Anna baby, I need you to calm down."* Bishop said to Anna. He had just explained to her that he was going back into the game in an effort to save Quinton.

*"How the hell do you expect me to calm down Byron?!"* Anna yelled. *"You just told me that you are going to start selling drugs. Drugs Byron!"*

*"It's for my son Anna."* Bishop said quietly as he watched Anna pace back and forth.

*"I am so tired of hearing that! Everything is always for Quinton. Guess what? You have a daughter too! Or have you forgotten? Hell you barely pay her any attention as it is!"* she screamed at him as she started throwing anything that she could get her hands on.

*"Don't do that!"* Bishop said. *"I love Traniece and you. You know that. I don't have to worry about Traniece because I know that she is doing what she is supposed to be doing. But I have had MANY conversations with our daughter about her missing her brother Anna.*

165

*Many conversations. So don't sit there and tell me that I don't communicate with her."* He said sternly.

*"No. Don't give me that shit! You always jump whenever Quinton does something. If he wants to go out there and mess up his life, let him. He is a grown man. We can't keep being punished because he's a screw up!"* Anna yelled. She realized what she said and watched Bishop's facial expression change.

Bishop couldn't believe what he had heard. All the times that he felt like Anna was handling it well. Maybe there was some truth to what Tanya was saying about Quinton being uncomfortable here, he thought.

*"Well, at least I know how you really feel."* He said as she tried to apologize for her words. *So because he came from another woman and not you he's a screw up? If my memory serves me correctly, you weren't always an angel either. But you act as if you never were on the bad side. You act like you've been the perfect first lady your whole life when we both know, you were getting down just like I was. But in eighteen years you can't accept the fact that I have a*

son that I actually want to take care of. That is my son damn it! Regardless of whether you want to acknowledge it or not, he's not going anywhere. I am bringing my son home, no matter what it takes!" he yelled angrily.

"Well you can do it without me. I don't want any part of it." Anna said with tears flowing down her face. She kneeled down under the bed and grabbed a suitcase, then started throwing clothes in the bag.

"Where are you going Anna?" Bishop asked her trying to regain his composure.

"I'm leaving." Anna said now throwing her belongings into the suitcase. "When you come to your senses, you know how to reach me." She grabbed her suitcase and walked to the door.

Bishop grabbed her arm as she walked by. "Anna please. Don't do this. Please try to understand." He pleaded.

A tear fell down Anna's face as she looked at her husband before walking out the door. "Goodbye Bishop."

Anna walked out the door and Bishop sat down on the bed. He didn't want it to come to this. He knew his decision would come with some consequences, but he didn't want to lose his wife. He placed his head into his hands and began to sob.

*"Daddy?"* he heard Traniece say. He looked up to see her standing at the doorway.

*"Hey baby. I thought, you went with your mother."* He said wiping his eyes. It seemed like lately, Traniece was seeing him at his worst rather than the man that usually has it together.

*"No. She came in and told me that she was leaving and I told her that I wanted to stay here with you."* She said.

Bishop looked at his daughter with confusion. *"Why? Baby I'm about to be involved in some heavy stuff and I can't have you or your mom being put at risk."* He said.

*"I know."* She said. *"I know the reason that you're doing it. Mom knows too, I think it's just hard for her to deal with because she feels like she keep reliving it."* She told him. *"I don't blame you for what you are about to do daddy. I know that you won't let anything*

168

*happen to Quinton or me. I believe that."*

Bishop wiped his tears and looked at his daughter lovingly. *"Thank you baby girl. Things are really about to get dangerous, and daddy is about to do some things that you may not really understand or like. But I need you to know that I love you no matter what, and I will protect both you and your brother with everything in my power."* He told her as he hugged her close.

*"I know daddy. I know. I feel like, in a twisted way, God answered my prayer."* She told him wiping her own eyes.

*"What do you mean baby girl?"* Bishop asked her.

*"I prayed to God that you would find a way to bring Quinton home. As wrong as it may seem, it's exactly what I asked for."* She said to her father.

Traniece got up to hug her father. *"I love you daddy, and I am praying that God keeps you safe through this."*

Bishop hugged his daughter tight. *"I love you too baby."* He watched his daughter walked back to her room feeling like what he was about to do was definitely the right thing.

*

## Chapter Six

Quinton and Read stepped out the hotel and walked towards the town car that was waiting to take them to meet with the connect that Read had been telling him about. The two got in the car and the driver began taking them to their destination. Read was giving him the run down on the connect and what to expect.

*"You really gotta be alert."* Read was telling him as they continued their drive. *"Don't ask him a lot of questions. If he thinks that you're grilling him then he will shut everything down. Just let me do the talking. If he asks you anything, don't pop off and say anything disrespectful. Dom has a lot of money and power. He can put us on the map kid."* He said.

*"I got you bruh."* Quinton said shaking his head in agreement. *"So is it gonna be a problem if I'm there? I know Ahmad usually goes with you and I'm assuming that is probably who he's used to dealing with."* He asked.

*"Nah man, you good."* Read told him. *"I done told him about*

*you before and he keeps his eyes and ears on anyone that's dealing with his product. He knows that you're over the Soldiers now and that I want to put you in charge of the warehouse."*

Quinton looked at him in surprise. *"Word? The warehouse? Yo that's wassupbruh!"*

Read stopped Quinton from getting too excited. *"Well look bruh I want to put you there but, I need you to be in 100% in kid. So I was gonna wait until you finished school so that I can make sure that you don't have any distractions."* He told him.

*"Ok cool. Well I guess I can hold off a few weeks. Now back to this Dom cat."* Quinton asked. *"Do I need to keep this or are they going to strip me the minute that I hit the door?"*he asked as he lifted up his shirt to reveal his burner tucked away neatly in his pants. .

Read laughed at his inquisitiveness. *"Yo, he's gonna expect you to have that on you. If you don't, he's gonna think it's a set up. Yo PK this ain't no BET made, shoot em up movie. We going in here to break bread with him. Calm down."*

Quinton shook his head in agreement as the driver

approached a very large black steel gate with the initials D.D. in them. The driver pulled to the front of the gate where a large key pad sat with a mounted camera to observe all visitors in and out of the mansion. Read was relaxed checking his phones but Quinton was looking at everything around him. He marked the two men standing at the front gate as they opened and the driver took the route up the mile long driveway in which they were greeted with a mansion that appeared to be the size of a small college campus. The driver pulled the car to the front door where a white man in a black suit greeted the two upon opening the door.

*"Greetings sirs."* The man said. *"Mr. Davis has been expecting you."* The two got out of the car and followed the man up the steps and into the home. Quinton was in amazement but he didn't let it show on his face in the event that he was being watched. The butler led the two to a large room where everything was decked out in white from the carpet to the furniture.

*"Please, make yourselves comfortable. Mr. Davis will be with you shortly."* He said as the two sat down on the couch. The butler left the room to inform Dom that his guests had arrived. A few

seconds later a young girl came into the room.

*"Can I get you anything to drink?"* she asked.

*"Bring them both three shots of bourbon, top shelf."* A voice said entering the room. The two looked up to see Dom entering the room. *"Fellas. I see that you finally made it."* He said. Read stood to greet Dom and Quinton followed his lead.

*"What's good Dom?"* Read greeted him dapping him up. The two remained in a close grip for a few seconds as Quinton stood observing. Dom stepped back and Quinton sized him up.

Dom stood to be about six foot five inches tall around 285 pounds. He appeared to be mixed as light as his complexion was. He assumed since he lived in Costa Rica that he had some type of Hispanic heritage. He was what Quinton considered to be a pretty boy with the pretty hair pulled back into a ponytail and his eyes a light hazel color. *How the hell did he come up?* He thought to himself. *He can't be that much older than me or Read.* He walked up to Dom and extended his hand for him to shake.

*"So you must be Q."* Dom said as he dapped Quinton up. *"I*

*have heard a lot about you. You are just like I thought you would be*

*man."* He said. *"Ya'll sit down and chill. Looking like you nervous or*

*some shit. Damn Read, what the hell you tell this dude about me?"* he

asked with a laugh.

Read laughed at Dom as the young girl reappeared with

several shot glasses of bourbon as Dom had requested. She placed

the glasses in front of each of them as Quinton listened to the

conversation at hand.

*"Man you gotta remember, he a PK. He was all sheltered and*

*shit. His pops quit hustling after he was born and shit."* He said.

*"That's right. Bishop is your father. What a coincidence. Yea*

*he and my family go way back."* Dom said with a smile on his face. *"I*

*heard he's an actual Bishop now. How is that going for him?"* he

asked.

*"Its fine."* Quinton answered shortly.

Dom smirked. *"It's a shame. Guess he couldn't cut it."* He

said studying Quinton's face. Quinton's jaw clinched but he said

nothing. Knowing that he pissed him off, Dom smiled. *"So you following in daddy's footsteps huh?"*

Quinton looked at Read who was giving him a look of warning. Ignoring it, Quinton looked Dom directly in the eye and said *"I ain't my father. My name is Q. Not Bishop."* He put his hands in his lap as he sat back in case he had to make a quick decision.

Read looked a little uneasy for a minute until Dom began to laugh. Reads face relaxed and he began to laugh as well.

*"I like this one Read."* He said giving Read his approval. *"That's what I need. Let's drink fellas."* He picked up a shot of bourbon and drank. Quinton and Read did the same. They drank until there was no more and the young girl who stood silently in the corner came and collected the empty glasses. She exited quickly leaving the men alone to talk.

*"Now lets get down to business."* Dom said. He sat across from Read and Quinton and pulled papers out from a covered tray that was on the table. *"I got a new product that will put these nickel and dimers out on the streets, permanently."* He said as he unfolded the papers. *"I have a few already trying to put it on the streets but its*

*getting harder to get this shit into the states with all these newbies tryna follow the rules and shit. I'm working on getting that taken care of with some people that owe me. But when this shit hit, I need ya'll to make this shit your muthafucking priority."* He said.

Read and Quinton were both curious. Quinton spoke first. *"So what is it that you need from us? You tryna get us to smuggle the shit in or something?"* he asked suspiciously.

Dom looked at Quinton as if he was stupid. *"I don't just trust anyone with my money."* He said. *"Did I ask you to bring my shit? No. I said make my shit priority. Listen to my words before I change my mind on you boy."*

Quinton was trying to keep composure but Dom was starting to get under his skin. Read sensing Quinton's frustration jumped in. *"Alright bruh we got you. So what you need us to do? We on it."*

Dom looked at Quinton and back to Read. *"You better be right about him. O quees un hombre muerto."* He said.

*"Yo no tomodemasiadobien a lasamenazas."* Quinton said

letting Dom know that he understood his threatening his life in

Spanish. *"En el juego, sabe con quienestatratando con."*

Dom stood surprised and impressed at the young boys knowledge.

*"Impressive. Follow me."*

*

Bishop had been driving aimlessly for the past two hours all

over Atlanta. He had found himself driving to some of his old hang

out spots where he and his boys use to hang out and hustle. He had

left Duece's house not too long ago where Duece had given him all

the information on what Quinton was involved in. Bishop told

himself that he wasn't going to get completely back into the game,

but just enough to where he could get close. Bishop continued to

drive and decided to stop at Tanya's to tell her what was going on

and the decision that he had made. He pulled up to her house and

called her cell phone.

*"Hello?"* she answered.

*"Hey it's me. I'm outside your house."* He said.

*"Okay. What's going on? Why do you sound so out of it?"* she asked him genuinely concerned.

*"Do you mind if I come in?"* he asked her.

*"Yea of course. Come on it. I'm gonna unlock the door and throw some clothes on."* She said.

*"Alright."* He hung up the phone and walked to her door to find it unlocked as she had said. He went over to her bar and fixed himself a drink and sat down on her recliner chair.

*"Well this must be serious for you to have a drink in your hand."* She said as she entered the room. Tanya came in the room wearing an oversized tee shirt and some blue jean leggings. Her hair was pulled into a messy bun with wisps of hair falling all over her head.

Bishop sighed and closed his eyes as he lie his head back onto the chair. Tanya grabbed a bottle of water and sat down on the love seat next to the chair.

*"So what's going on?"* she asked him. She had never seen

Bishop so flustered so she was starting to be really concerned.

Bishop massaged his temples and let everything out. *"A lot has happened in these last couple of days Tanya. Ever since the other night, stuff has just been off course. I left here and I lied to my wife about where I was. I haven't lied to my wife in so long. And I don't wanna hurt her again more than I already have. I mean I may have omitted a few details but I have never just flat out lied to her."* He said frustrated.

Tanya sat looking confused. *"Well Bishop, not to be funny but, keeping details from your wife is kind of the same thing as lying. I'm not tryna tell you that you're not trying, and I'm not throwing shade but, there's been a lot of deceit in some form."* She said.

*"True."* He agreed. *"But I just didn't want to intentionally hurt her. Then we got into this big argument and when I woke up the next morning, someone had thrown a brick through the windshield of my car."* He said.

*"Oh my God! Who would do that? Why would they do that?"* she asked upset.

Bishop hesitated to tell her the next part. *"Well, there was also a note attached to the brick. Basically it was threatening Quinton's life."* He watched Tanya's expression and saw the color drain from her face.

*"What?"* she asked to reaffirm what she believed that she heard. *"What do you mean threatened his life?! Bishop what the hell are you talking about?"*

Bishop leaned forward to try to calm her down. *"It was a note attached to the brick that said that I should prepare myself for his death. But you know I'm not going to let anything happen to our son."* He took a deep breath. *"Which is why I called Duece."*

Tanya's expression went from upset to pissed off. *"You what?!"* she asked. *"Bishop what the hell is wrong with you? You went through all that drama to get out the streets and now you're tryna go back in? This ain't like it was 18 years ago. Bishop these little boys are out here killing people without blinking. I can only imagine what Anna thought!"* she yelled.

*"Tanya calm down. Its not like I'm just doing this because.*

*It's the only way I can think of to save Quinton. Would you much rather he get killed and I do nothing about it?"* he asked her.

*"No! But Bishop what you are doing is dangerous. What did Anna say?"* she asked.

*"She left. For lack of better words, she didn't feel as if what I was doing was worth it."* He said knowing that she was about to go off. *"So she said that she wasn't going to stick around and left. She tried to take Traniece with her but she told her that she wanted to stay with me."*

Tanya was a ball of emotions. *"What the hell you mean that she didn't think it was worth it? See that's the shit I was talking about! My son isn't worth you saving? I mean I don't necessarily agree with the shit but, if it's a way to save our son, she doesn't understand? That bitch better be glad that I didn't see her. How the hell could she even form her fucking lips to even say that about my son? I'm so sick of this shit!"* she said. She walked over to the bar, poured her a shot and took it straight down.

*"Look Tanya calm down. I pretty much told her the same*

*thing that you did. I don't think that she meant to say it like that. I just think that she was worried about me going back in is all."* He told her to try to smooth over the situation. *"She just needs some time to calm down."* He said.

*"Whatever. Like I said, she better be glad I wasn't there cause her ass would've got drug. Now what did Duece say?"* she asked.

Bishop poured himself another drink and told her everything as he sipped. *"Well, when I went over there, I filled him in on how I thought he was working with Read. So apparently Read is still over the Soldiers as he was when I left all those years ago. He said that Read has opened up quite a few shops in town. He bought a couple houses in the area and a large house in Peachtree. Quinton started running but from what Duece was saying, Read put him in charge of the Soldiers and security. Apparently the boy Ray Ray that was handling it was messing up and Quinton called him out. Quinton is becoming to Read what Read was to me. They left for Costa Rica yesterday and I tried to tell him not to go."* He said.

*"You talked to him?"* Tanya asked.

"Yea. I called Read to try to talk to him but of course, all Read was thinking about was money." He said. "Quinton called me a few minutes later and told me that he wasn't quitting."

"Wait a minute." Tanya said interrupting him. "You said that they were going to Costa Rica? But the only thing there is..."

"Dom." Bishop finished her thought. "Yea I know. But Duece has got an eye on Read and I'm about to get a few people together to get close to him. So I am going to be under him, but he just won't know." He told her. "Tanya I swear that seeing what Quinton is doing is like looking in a mirror. I have to stop him before it gets too bad." he said.

Tanya looked at Bishop and saw how serious he was. "Well, I cant say that I'm completely crazy about the idea Bishop. This is some dangerous stuff you're about to get into." She felt the lump forming in her throat as she was speaking. "But if it's going to save Quinton, then...do it. I'm with you."

"Thank you." He said. "I'm glad you agree."

"That's why I want in." she told him.

184

Bishop looked at her like she was crazy. *"Tanya have you lost your mind? This isn't some game. This is some dangerous stuff. What do I look like asking the mother of my child to do something illegal? Think about your job. Think about Quinton. What if I were to get caught? Or you? Its not going to do us any good for Quinton if both of us were in jail. No. Out of the question."* He told her.

Tanya was not backing down. *"I know the risks. But I also know that my son is not going to go willingly as if the last six months was in vain. Truthfully, we both know that he has been doing this longer than six months. You and I both know this. But I am not about to let you do this by yourself. I still have a few connections as well, or have you forgotten who you were dealing with?"*

Bishop smirked. Tanya had always been about business when he met her. She was one of the best females in the game, and in fact, better than most of his squad. She knew how to make the money with nothing leading back to her. He knew he wasn't going to be able to talk her out of it. He admired the fact that she still had a little bit of the street in her despite the fact that she was a practicing doctor. He stared at her long and hard. *"Alright."* He said. *"But if this gets too bad, I'm pulling you out.*

*"Trust me, I wont get too close."* She said. *"Thank you."* she said a few seconds later.

*"For what?"* he asked her.

*"For understanding."* She said as she walked over to hug him.

The two embraced in a long hug and she looked up to see his big brown eyes looking down at her. Both were starting to get the feeling that they had the last time they were together. Bishop spoke first.

*"We cant do this again Tanya. What happened the other night, shouldn't have happened."* He said as he released her from his grasp.

*"I know."* She said reluctantly. *"I know. I know that I don't necessarily like Anna but, I don't want to be the other woman either. It was just, a lot of feelings came back that I thought I had suppressed and well, obviously they did for you too."* She said as she

looked at him in a hopeful manner.

Bishop sighed knowing that deep down that he still cared for Tanya but he truly loved Anna. He just had such a strong physical attraction to Tanya and she was the one that understood his every thought. She let him be him without any nagging or complaints. All she ever asked was that he have a relationship with his son.

*"So you do still have feelings."* She said snapping him out of his thoughts.

*"Yes Tanya I do."* He admitted. *"But I'm married. I'm always going to care about you because you are the mother to my only son."* Bishop was lying to her and himself, but he didn't want to get anything extra started. Right now, he just needed to focus on his son and getting to him before it was too late.

*"Ok."* Tanya said. *"I'm not going to harp on it. Quinton is the main priority right now."* She said. Bishop could tell that although she was dropping it, she had not let it go completely.

*"Alright so, what's the first move?"* she asked. Bishop walked over to her mini bar and poured himself a drink to fill her in on his

plan.

*

Quinton walked out on to the balcony of the villa where he was staying in Costa Rica. He was taking the evening to relax while and enjoy the country before he went back to Atlanta the next day. The meeting that he and Read had with Dom had started off a little rocky but, Quinton had the feeling that he had earned Dom's respect and trust. Dom had set them up to make a nice piece of money and Quinton planned on hustling as hard as he could. He was still dealing with graduating in a few weeks and he wanted to hurry to finish so that he could take over the warehouse that Read had mentioned to him. Just thinking about it, Quinton got excited. He didn't really want to walk with his class but, he knew that his sister and mother wanted it.

He was about to grab a beer when he heard a knock at his door. He walked over to the door to see that the personal concierge that was assigned to his room was coming to check on him. He opened the door to find a girl who appeared to be in her early twenties standing in a black fitted dress that stopped mid knee level. He was guessing that she was around a size 6 frame with an ass that made Kim Kardashian look like she had small mosquito bites. Quinton flashed her his winning smile as she stood awaiting his command.

*"Good evening sir. I am Roxanna and I will be serving you during your stay here. Is there anything that I can get for you? Are you finding the villa to your liking?"* she asked him.

*"Oh I am enjoying everything that I see here love. And please, call me Q. Come on in."* he told her. He stepped to the side so that she could enter the room. He watched her walk in and closed the door behind her. *Damn she's bad.,* he thought to himself. He felt his manhood start to harden just looking at her.

*"So may I get you anything?"* she asked him with a smile.

Quinton smiled at the thought of what she could serve him. *"Baby what I want, is definitely not something that can be given to me on a tray."* He looked at her body up and down and gave her a menacing smile. He could tell that she was understanding what he was hinting at because she walked to the table to put her empty tray down.

*"And what sir is it that you want?"* she asked seductively.

Quinton grinned at how easy his request was and slowly took off his wife beater revealing his bare chest. The crucifix that he wore around his neck stood out against his chocolate skin. He walked over towards Roxanna and placed his arms around her pulling her to him. He felt her body pressed against him and his manhood grew pushing against her body to show her his impressive sized package. He leaned down to her short figure and began kissing her slowly on her neck bringing his lips to hers. He kissed her lips passionately as he pulled the straps down on her dress revealing her perfect size 36 D cup breasts. The two begin to kiss as if there was nothing left to do. He cupped her breasts in his hands and began to slowly circle her nipple with his tongue making her purr in satisfaction. She began fumbling with his belt buckle pulling his pants down and seeing the bulge in his boxer briefs. She dropped to her knees and placed him into her mouth and began to suck him as if she were thirsty and needed her thirst quenched.

*"Shit."* Quinton moaned in pleasure as she continued to place him deeper and deeper into her waiting throat. He could practically feel her tonsils touching the tip of his dick she was putting him so far down her throat. He thrust himself in her mouth over and over as she moaned and groaned enticing him even more. *"Damn most girls would've been gagging on the dick."* He said to her as she sucked him like a pro.

He pulled her up to her feet and walked her towards the bed. He threw her on top of the covers and took her dress of revealing her in a thong. He knelt down and spread her legs wide and began kissing her inner thighs, teasing her as he caressed her with his tongue in every spot except her pearl. She begged for him to taste her and after a few more moments of teasing, he devoured her as if she were a steak dinner. He continued to eat her as she screamed over and over.

Quinton smiled as she climaxed multiple times and stood over her pulling his massive manhood out to enter her. He placed the condom on and pushed his way inside of her stretching her walls and making her cry out. The two begin to kiss as he thrust himself in and out of her slowly. She began to cry out.

*"Oh dios se sientebien!"* she yelled as she dug her fingernails into his back. She pushed him up to let him know that she wanted to change positions. He lay on his back while she climbed on top of him riding hi backwards so that he could watch her ass bounce and jiggle as he thrust deeper and deeper into her with each stroke. He smacked her hard on her right cheek making her scream his name.

*"Q!"* she yelled. *"Aye papi!"* he gripped her cheeks as she continued to bounce up and down.

*"Tegustaeste dick!"* Quinton yelled.

*"Si papi! Por favor, no deje de mi, carajo!"* she said as she came again.

Quinton picked her up placing her on all fours and she immediately arched her back ready for him to take her in her favorite position. He grabbed her long hair and wrapped it around his hand as he pounded her walls making her scream until there were nothing but silent cries. His strokes become slower and deeper as he felt himself about to reach his peak. He gripped her waist harder and felt her body beginning to tremble beneath him. A few seconds later he followed suit pulling out of her and watching his work smash against the condom.

Roxanna lay there with her body convulsing from the multiple orgasms that Quinton had given her in the last hour. She turned to see that he was beginning to doze off. She quietly got up to go to the bathroom to clean herself up. She closed the bathroom door behind her turning on the water and quickly washed herself and noticed his jewelry sitting on the counter. She grabbed two of his rings clasping them tightly in her hand. She cut the water off that drowned out the sound of her getting dressed and opened the door to find Quinton standing there. She jumped and tried to regain composure.

*"You scared me."* She said as she tried to walk past him.

Quinton looked at her and smiled knowing that something was up.

*"So....arent you supposed to be my personal assistant?"* he asked her. *"I haven't dismissed you yet."* He told her.

Roxanna smiled a fake smile and giggled. *"Yes sir. What would you like?"*

Quinton's smiled disappeared quickly as he answered. *"You can give me back the two rings that you just stole off my damn counter."* He said blocking her way to the door.

Roxanna tried to play it off as if she didn't know what he was talking about. *"What do you mean? I haven't taken anything."* She said folding her arms across her chest and secretly sliding the rings into her bra.

Quinton grabbed her by her arm dragging her out the bathroom door.

*"Let go of me!"* she demanded. *"You're hurting me."*

He dragged her in front of his television cutting it on to show her on camera. *"If you work here then you would know that I requested a room with cameras. So its obvious that you don't work here. Hand it over."* He said as he held his hand out.

Realizing that she had no other option, she reached into her bra giving him his jewelry.

*"Sit down."* He told her pointing to the chair in the corner. *"Who sent you?"* he asked her.

*"Nobody."* She responded not wanting to give herself up.

Quinton slapped her across the face. Roxanna cried out in pain. He leaned forward grabbing her by her throat. *"Now I'm going to ask you one more time before I snap your fucking neck. Who sent you?"*

A single tear rolled down her face. *"Dom."* She answered.

Quinton stood up straight at the mention of his name. *"Dom? What the fuck he fucking with me for?"* he asked. *"So what were you supposed to do huh? Fuck for some jewelry?"*

*"No."* She said. *"He sent me to steal the bricks he gave you. He wanted me to set you up so that way he could get rid of you."*

Quinton let her go and walked away towards the drawer by the bed. He pulled the gun out. *"So what were you stealing the jewelry for?"* he asked.

*"Payment."* She said. *"He told me to take what I wanted. Im sorry."* She pleaded as she saw him coming towards her with the gun.

*"Yea well, your plan backfired. But you can give him a message."* He said.

*"What?"* she asked.

*"This."* He said as he fired a single bullet in between her eyes silencing her permanently. Her head fell back as blood began to pour. He pulled out his cell phone and called Read.

*"Wassup PK?"* Read answered.

*"I need clean up. I'll explain it later."* He responded into the phone.

*"Where you at?"* Read asked.

*"The Villa."* Quinton said.

*"Aight. On the way."* Read said.

Quinton hung up the phone and began to throw all of his stuff into a large duffel bag. He recalled what she had just told him.

*"Muthafuckas bout to know Q."* he said.

\*

## Chapter Seven

Bishop went into the church early in the morning before the maintenance was scheduled to come in. He felt like he was in the calm before the storm and he wanted to get his thoughts to the altar. He knelt before the altar and began to pray.

*"Father, I come to you as humbly as I know how. Lord, this is hard for me because I feel like I am being a hypocrite coming into Your house and asking you for forgiveness when I know that I'm probably going to go out there and do worse. Lord I know that you are tired of me apologizing but my son is a reminder of how far I have come and I don't want to lose him to the very thing that I got caught up in. Father I ask that you please watch over me as well as my family during this very trying time. Especially Tanya, we both know that she is stubborn and doesn't want to step aside easily. Keep her safe so that if something does happen to me, she will be there for our son."* He prayed. He continued to silently pray when he heard the doors of the church open. He turned around to see a woman walking down the aisle towards him. As she got closer, he saw it was Alexis,

Miss Beece's granddaughter.

*"Alexis?"* he called out to her.

Alexis walked up to him as he got up from the altar. The closer that she got, he could tell that she had been crying.

*"I didn't think that I would find you here this early."* She told him as he embraced her in a hug.

*"Yea I normally am not here this early however I had a few things on my heart this morning that I needed to go to God with."* He told her as he motioned for her to sit on the pew.

*"Sounds like you and me both."* She told him as she felt the tears stinging her eyes.

Bishop saw how her face changed and got concerned. *"Hey, hey, hey what's wrong? What's going on?"* he asked her genuinely concerned.

Alexis took a deep breath before she completely broke down in tears. *"Grandma passed away last night!"* she sobbed almost falling out of the pew. Bishop grabbed her and held her to keep her from falling.

*"Okay, wait a minute. Slow down."* He told her as he tried to understand what she was saying. *"Okay now talk to me. What happened?"* he asked.

Alexis collected herself and spoke slowly. *"Last night, grandma passed away. Me and daddy went to visit her at the hospital and she asked us to go to the cafeteria to get her something to eat. We went down there and decided to stop at the gift shop to get her some flowers. When we got back, she was dead!"* she wailed. *"Apparently, while we were downstairs, she told the doctor that she was tired of dealing with it and wanted him to unplug her. We asked him why did he let her do it and he said he saw how tired she was and that he couldn't argue with her anymore. Why did she leave me?"* she cried out as she crumpled yet again.

Bishop grabbed her and hugged her close. *"Alexis I wish I knew what to say right now to ease your heart from this pain."* He said as she continued to cry on his shoulder. Bishop did the only thing that he knew how to do. *"Lord,"* he said *"Alexis is hurting right now from the loss of her grandmother. Father we know you that although she's not here in the physical sense, you called her home for a reason. Help her heal Lord. Help her and her family get through these tough times. Let your spirit surround her in these times ahead Father."* He prayed. Bishop continued to sit at the pew and hold Alexis as she wept.

*"Just let it out."* He said.

Alexis spoke out as in between sobs. *"I just don't want to believe it. She was like a mother to me."* She said as she began to slow her cries. *"She was the only one in my family that didn't make me feel like crap for the things I've done. She didn't judge me. She didn't make me feel like an outcast."* She said sniffling.

Bishop looked concerned with what she was telling him. *"What are you talking about?"* he asked her.

Alexis was about to speak when the door opened and they both turned to see three men enter the church. As they got closer, Bishop saw that it was the maintenance men that were there to fix the roof.

*"Good morning gentlemen."* He said as he looked at his

watch. He had not realized that an hour had already passed since he had been in the church. *"I'm assuming you are here to fix the roof?"* he asked.

*"Yes sir."* One of the men answered.

Bishop stood and motioned for Alexis to follow him. *"Well we will get out of your way."* He said as he watched one of the men staring at Alexis. *"Alexis do you want to continue this in my office?"* he asked her. Alexis shook her head in agreement and followed him to the office.

Bishop walked down the hallway ahead of Alexis and shed a few tears for Miss Beece. He thought about what she had told him on his last visit to the hospital. He got to the door and unlocked it cutting the light on. He stepped to the side so that Alexis could step in.

*"Come on in."* he said as he placed his keys on the desk. Alexis took a seat on the sofa that was in the corner and Bishop closed the door behind him sitting down at his desk.

*"Now you were telling me something about feeling like you*

*were an outcast?"* he asked her.

Alexis shook her head. *"Yea."* She took a couple of deep breaths and explained. *"When I was growing up, I didn't have my mother around. So my father took care of me with the help of my grandmother. I developed early as a child. My cousins used to always tease me about the way that I looked and I'm not gonna lie, I started messing with boys early. When my cousins found out, they made fun of me and called me a whore and everything that you could think of."* She paused as she felt tears forming again.

Bishop reached over to his desk to retrieve a box of tissues and handed them over to her.

*"What they didn't know is that my mothers husband was abusing me. I was told that the only thing I was good for was lying on my back."* Alexis started to get angry. *"I didn't know how to tell them but my father found out and told my grandmother. She told me that everything was going to be okay and that I didn't do anything wrong. As I got older, I did whatever I wanted to with whoever I wanted. I really didn't see anything wrong with what I was doing because I was*

*honest with them you know?"* she said. Bishop shook his head listening to everything that she was saying. *" I never lied to anybody and I always kept it 100 with them. I just am tired of having to cry all the time. My grandmother was all I had."* She told him as she let herself fall apart.

Bishop stood to walk over towards the couch. He sat next to her and grabbed her hand. *"Let me tell you something."* He said. *"Your grandmother is extremely proud of the woman that you are. Now granted, I have not known you your entire life, but I can tell that if Miss Beece had a hand in raising you, that you are an alright person and if you are anything like your grandmother, I know you are a strong woman."* He told her with a laugh.

Alexis smiled thinking about how stubborn her grandmother was. Her father always reminded her of how much like her that she was.

*"Yea that's true. It just...seems so surreal."* Alexis said. *"I knew that this was happening for a while. I just thought she would fight harder."* She gripped his hand harder and leaned on his

shoulder. *"Oh God!"* she cried. *"Please give her back!"*

Bishop rubbed her back with one hand and continued to hold her hand with the other as he attempted to soothe her. He was completely at a loss for words but he didn't want to leave her alone. He was supposed to meet Deuce but he was still a pastor. She looked up at him with tears streaming down her face and he felt himself starting to rise looking at her. Attempting to ignore his urge, he wiped the tears off her face. She looked at him and slowly leaned towards him kissing his lips. Bishop kissed her back, then realizing what he was doing, backed away.

*"Alexis, this is wrong. Your grandmother just passed and you're just reacting out of hurt."* He said to her. She placed her fingers over his lips.

*"Please."* She requested. *"Just, let me have this."*

Alexis kissed Bishop again while unzipping her jacket. She revealed her chest to him and began to kiss on his neck while she massaged his growing manhood. He lay her down on the couch on top of her and began to massage her breasts. She pulled her skirt up and Bishop unbuckled his pants. He slid her panties to the side and entered her quickly, pumping in and out of her with such force. Both were soothing each others hurt. They were giving each other temporary relief for their own bad situations. Bishop began to pump faster as he felt himself about to explode. He gripped her hand tightly as they both exploded. The two lay there on his couch for a few moments panting heavily trying to catch their breath. Bishop sat up as he looked down at Alexis. Quietly, they both began to fix their clothing and straighten up knowing that what they had just done was wrong.

*"I guess I should leave you to your business."* Alexis said as she zipped her jacket back up.

Bishop stood and went to sit back in his seat massaging the temples of his head. *What the hell did I just do?,* he thought to himself. *I just banged this girl in the church!* He thought. His head was spinning at the thought of what he had just done.

*"So will you do it?"* Alexis asked snapping him out of his thoughts.

*"I'm sorry. Do what?"* he asked.

*"I said that my dad and the rest of the family may need someone there to help them. And of course when the arrangements are being made I know they will want you to give the eulogy."* She said.

*"Oh of course."* He said. *"I will stop by later on this evening and check on the family."*

*"Thanks."* She said as she avoided looking him in the eyes. *"Ok well I have to go. Sorry about...you know."* She said as she left the office.

Alexis closed the door and rushed to her car leaving Bishop in the office. Bishop sat back in his chair and closed his eyes trying to figure out what was going on with him. *What the hell am I doing?* He thought to himself. He pulled out his cell phone and saw he had two missed calls one from Deuce and the other from Traniece. He called Traniece first.

*"Hey daddy."* She answered. Bishop immediately smiled when he heard his daughters voice.

"Hey baby girl." He said. "Im sorry I missed your call a while ago. What's up pumpkin?" He asked her.

"Well I just wanted to call you and remind you about the father daughter dance. Its next weekend and I know, this last month has been a little...crazy. We don't have to go if you don't want to." She said.

"Baby girl, not only will I take you, but I will be there in a tux." He told her reassuring her that he would be there for her. He could almost see her smiling on the other end.

"Ok daddy. Are you okay?" she asked him.

"Yea baby Im okay. I just needed to come to the church to make sure the maintenance men were in to fix the roof. I might be home a little late though because Miss Beece passed last night and I want to and visit the family." He told her.

"Oh no." she said sadly. "I'm sorry to hear about that. I'm going to go with you tonight. I was going to go and visit mom but I will make sure that I leave early enough." She said.

*"Okay baby girl that's fine."* He said.

*"Have you talked to mom?"* she asked him.

Bishop sighed. He missed Anna like crazy even though it didn't seem like it with the way that he had been acting lately.

*"I've tried to call her a few times but I don't think that she's ready to talk to me yet pumpkin"* he told her.

Bishop heard Traniece sigh on the phone.

*"Don't worry baby girl. I'm going to figure out a way to fix this."* He said as he ended his call. *"I love you baby girl and I will see you tonight."* He said hanging up.

Bishop looked at the time and contemplated calling Deuce but decided against it and grabbed his car keys to head over there. He walked out of his office locking the door and saw that his secretary was now in her office. *I wonder how long she's been here?* He thought. He peeked into her office and she glanced up at him over her glasses.

*"Good morning Bishop."* She said

*"Good morning sister Peters."* He greeted her. *"I didn't hear you come in."* he said fishing to see when she arrived.

*"Oh I haven't been here long. I had come in to be here for the repair men. Had I known you would be here honey I would have stayed in the bed."* She joked.

The two exchanged a laugh and satisfied with what he heard, Bishop said his goodbyes and headed to his car. When he was out of earshot, she picked up the phone to call her best friend.

*"Gladys honey you will not believe what I just saw."* She said as she began to tell her about Bishop's office rendezvous.

*

Quinton paced the floor waiting on Read to return from Dom's. He wanted to kill him for the shit that he had pulled sending the girl but Read said he was going to handle it. He had left early that morning and assured him that he would have everything straightened out, and now it was almost time for them to board their plane to head back to Atlanta. Quinton sat down on the bed and checked his cell phone. He saw that he had a text message from his sister so to keep himself from going crazy he decided to text her back.

Quinton: Wassup? I saw you texted me a bit ago.

Niecey: Hey I have a father daughter dance I'm supposed to go to, and I don't think that he can make it. Do you think that you can take me?

Quinton: When is it?

Niecey: Next Friday. Please Q? I ain't tryna roll up in there by myself.

Quinton: Aight I got you.

Niecey: ☺☺☺☺☺ Thank you!!!!

Quinton: Np. Where you at?

Niecey: On my way to school.

Quinton: Aight cool. I'll hit you up when I get back.

Niecey: Back? Back from where?

*Quinton: I'm out of town. But I'm on my way back today.*

*Niecey: Ok. Well just hit me when you get back.*

Quinton looked up from his phone when he heard the key unlocking the door. Read entered the room with a troubled look on his face.

"*Yo man, what the fuck happened?*" Quinton asked before he could get settled.

"*Man damn can I get through the door?*" Read said.

"*Man what the hell? Do you not realize what the fuck happened today? Your fucking connect sent some bitch up here to get me or my shit, the shit that he fucking gave us to sell, for him, she tries to steal so he can fucking kill me?! And Im supposed to be calm about this shit?!*" Quinton asked pissed off.

Read put his stuff down and went to the bathroom to clean his hands. He still had remnants of blood in his fingernails from dumping Roxanne's body.

"*Man look. I went to him to see what was up with that shit*

*after we got rid of old girl. He says that she was sent as a gift to you*
*because he was impressed and that the whole setting you up shit was*
*a lie. I don't know if that nigga was lying or not because he act like*
*the chic was like his bottom bitch or something. He got all pissed off*
*and shit and the nigga started going ham when I told him you iced*
*the bitch. Shit I had to calm that nigga down and explain to him that*
*she told you she was there to set you up. All this pussy around here*
*and he act like she was golden or some shit."* He said as he replayed
the conversation to his friend. What he didn't tell him was that
Dom still had a vendetta against his father and wanted to get as
close to Bishop as possible.

*"He's just mad I fucked his bitch."* Quinton said. *"Probably*
*fucked her better than him."*

*"Look bruh. Lets just pack the rest of this shit up, cut this trip*
*short, head back to the A, and make this money. With the bricks that*
*he gave us, this could be the beginning of a big set up man. I'm*
*talking about millions in a matter of weeks! I need you with me on*
*this bruh."* Read said letting Quinton know that he was on his side.

Quinton grabbed his things and headed to the door. *"You ain't said nothing but a word. Let's go make this money."*

*

Bishop sat in Duece's living room in front of five of his friends that he used to run with as well as a group of young boys that he and Deuce had recruited the last couple of weeks. Everyone sat in the room in all black as if it were a scene out of New Jack City. Tanya sat by his side in all black as well. Deuce stood in the middle of the room and spoke.

*"Aight yall listen up."* He said. *"For the young niggas here in the room, you are sitting in front of greatness. To the right of this beautiful lady is Bishop. Bishop is the reason why we are all eating today. Together, me and Bishop started the Soldiers and made it great. But now, the Soldiers are falling apart. Their own egos are getting in the way of them making money. They're too busy chasing pussy or showing off rather than chasing this money."* Deuce said disgusted.

Bishop looked around to see everyone in the room hanging on

to Deuce's every word. He stood up to talk.

"What's worse, is that my son is involved. We all know
Quinton, and knows that he's a good boy. But, unfortunately, Read,
the one that I brought up personally in this game, is now bringing my
son into his mess. I have to put a stop to that no matter what the
cost. I walked away from the life I've known in the church to save him
and I'm not stopping until he is home." He said to the group.

"So what you want us to do?" one of Bishops old friends Dice
asked.

"We hit them off at the pass." Tanya said interjecting. "We
get their bricks before they can get them out on the streets. We bout
to hit them and take them for everything." She said.

"The first move is to hit up their trap houses in the area."
Bishop said. "Now Read and Quinton are in Cuba and supposedly are
having a meeting with Dom. Now Dom is becoming a problem now,
just like his father was years ago. So we have to show Dom that we
mean business and that we still run this. So Friday, we hit the house
in Bankhead." Bishop told everybody.

The group shook their heads to show that they understood followed by a slew of *"cools"* and *"that's wassup."*

Deuce came back to the center of the group. "Now look. We want to try to do this quick and quiet without much noise. I ain't saying go out and kill everybody in sight but, do what needs to be done." He said.

Bishop felt his phone going off in his pocket. He pulled it out to see an incoming text message from Anna. He immediately opened it and read her message.

*Wife: So...u had sex with some random girl in your office? Is this part of saving your son?*

*"Oh shit."* Bishop said. Everyone in the room turned to Bishop to see what's wrong.

*"What's good Bishop?"* Deuce asked looking confused.

Bishop looked up to see everyone looking at him. *"Uh....nothing. Everything is straight. I just need to go make a phone call."*

Bishop got up to walk outside and hit the speed dial to call his wife. It rang several times before she picked up.

*"What the hell do you want adulterer? Huh? You've got some nerve calling me!"* Anna screamed into the phone.

*"Anna please baby. Try to calm down. What are you talking about?"* he asked her to stall for time to come up with a lie for whatever she was about to tell him.

*"Are you serious right now?"* she asked. *"So you're gonna sit there, wherever the hell you are and tell me that you didn't have sex with some random hoe at the church?! In your office? Newsflash Byron, your secretary called Gladys, who then made it her mission to call my mother who then called me. Now damn near all of Atlanta probably knows about what you did! You fucked a bitch in your office!"* she screamed into the phone.

Bishop stood outside on the phone pacing trying to think quickly on his feet.

*"Baby I'm sorry. It wasn't like I planned it."* Bishop said. *"I honestly didn't. I went to the church because I wanted to just clear*

217

*my head and she came in there telling me about her grandmother. She was upset so I invited her to my office to relax and it just happened. Baby I swear I wasn't looking for anything to happen.* " He pleaded.

"*You didn't mean for anything to happen?!*" she yelled again. "*Did you mean to stop it? Cause you damn sure could've stopped her Byron. But you didn't. Did you think about how this would affect your family? No. And to do it in the church? What kind of sick shit is that? Yea that's real Christian like.*" She said.

"*I know. I know. Anna baby, I swear, I did not mean for it to happen. Everything is just going so fast lately and I don't know what to do.*" He said.

"*And you know Byron, I was actually coming around to this whole you trying to save your son thing. But sex, has absolutely nothing to do with your son. Sex is just you being selfish! I'm tired of it! Its been 23 years and I'm still dealing with the same bull!*" she said crying in the phone.

"*Baby I'm sorry. Just, tell me what I need to do to make this* right. I swear this wont happen again. I know that I've fallen off the path that I was led on right now, but, I cant live my life without you. Please, just tell me what I need to do." Bishop begged.

"Oh you wanna know what you can do? You can give me a divorce because I'm done!" she yelled.

Bishop stared at his phone to see his screen saver of the picture of Quinton and Traniece, which indicated his wife had hung up.

"So you had sex with another girl?" Bishop turned around to see Tanya standing at the door. It appeared as if she had heard the entire conversation.

Bishop sighed not wanting to deal with what was to come.

"Tanya please. Now is not a good time." He said.

"What do you mean now is not a good time?" she asked as she stepped down the stairs towards him. "How can you even do something like that when we are trying to get our son back? I see some things never change." She said.

Bishop threw his hands up. "Tanya what do you want me to do?

*What do you want me to say? You just heard me on the phone. My marriage is over! She wants a divorce!"*

*"Well what do you expect? I don't blame her! You said that you were in this for your son, when you are in this for yourself."* She accused him.

Bishop hung his head looking defeated. *"I don't know what to do anymore. I feel like everything is falling apart. I don't know what to say or do. I don't know who's on my side."* He said as he flopped down on the step.

*"Did you at least use protection with this girl?"* Tanya asked him.

Bishop sighed again and said *"I don't remember."*

*"Wow."* Tanya said. *"You clearly don't give a damn about anything. Hell I don't even think you care about actually saving your son."* She said.

Bishop grabbed her slamming her against the wall of the house. *"Don't you ever fucking say some shit like that again! Quinton is my son and I love him! I would die for him."* He said through gritted teeth.

*"Then act like it."* She said as she broke from his grasp and walked away back into the house.

*"Damn it."* He said. *"This has got to stop and now."* He said as he walked back into the house to put his plan into action.

\*

## Chapter Eight

Quinton and Read were stepping off the plane at the private airport and headed towards Lil G who was waiting for them in Reads Benz.

*"Yo whats good?"* Lil G asked. *"How was the trip man?"* he asked excited to see his boys.

*"Whats good man?"* Quinton said dapping him up. Lil G grabbed Reads bags and put them in the trunk of the car hopping in the backseat. Quinton got in the passenger seat and Read got behind the wheel.

*"So whats good bruh?"* Lil G asked. *"How was Cuba?"*

Quinton was looking out the window and decided to stay quiet to let Read answer.

*"It was great man. We got that new killa man. This shit gone have us set for life."* Read answered.

Lil G was excited to hear this because he was all about making money. *"Ya'll didn't have no problems or nothing did you?"* he asked making sure that he didn't have to go murk somebody. Quinton was like a big brother and Read was like his father.

Quinton looked at Read after hearing Lil G's question. *"Nah nothing we couldn't handle."* He answered.

They continued to drive to Bankhead to the trap house to make sure that everything was running smoothly. They had been gone for almost two weeks and Quinton wasn't trying to be do check-ups the next day because he promised Niecey he would take her to the father-daughter dance at her school. He decided to text Tierra to let her know that they were back.

*Quinton: Hey we are back. Meet me at the Bankhead spot. We are about to have a meeting.*

*Tierra: Aight. Be there in about 20 minutes.*

*Quinton: Coolin. Make sure to tell your girls to bring everything. No bullshit today.*

*Tierra: Aightbae I got you. Love you!* ☺

*Quinton: Ly2*

Quinton was starting to get annoyed with Tierra. When he first met her, she seemed real hardcore. She didn't get close to anybody and gave him a hard time. Now she seemed so clingy and despite the fact that she had some banging head game, she was always bothering him and being emotional. He decided he was going to let her go and soon. It was too many females out there for him and he was too young to be tied down. He felt his phone vibrate again in his lap and looked down assuming it was Tierra. He looked down to see that it was Maxine. She was still being hard to get but he was slowly starting to break her.

*Maxine: So I see you RSVP'd for Senior Day.*

Quinton smiled as he replied.

*Quinton: Yea I will be there. I get a chance to see your beautiful face right?*

*Maxine: Really? Smh....*

*Quinton: What? I'm just being honest.*

*Maxine: Uh huh.*

*Quinton: Besides, you know you wanted to talk to me anyway...*

*Maxine: Feeling yourself aren't you?*

*Quinton: I'd rather be feeling you.*

*Maxine: Bye Quinton.*

Read pulled up to the trap house and got out to head up the walkway. Lil G and Quinton followed behind him. They all walked in the house and Quinton hit the lights on his way in.

*"Surprise!"* he looked up to see all of his friends and Soldiers standing in the room in front of a big Congrats Grad banner. Quinton burst into a grin as he looked around to see all of his boys there.

*"Damn man. Ya'll got a nigga man."* Quinton said beaming as he went and greeted everybody. He dapped his boys up and gave all of his homegirls hugs. The music turned on and everybody started dancing and singing along with it. Quinton's favorite song came on and he began singing along to it as he danced with one of

his friends.

*Throwing money in the air like I don't really care*

*Standing on the chair like I don't really care*

*Got bitches by the pair, I'm baller of the year*

*And haters everywhere but, I don't really care.*

*WakaFlocka, I keep them bad bitches yelling it*

*Thugged out rich as hell plus I'm throwing dick*

*Drunk as shit*

*Everywhere I go I'm yelling "Bricksquad Monopoly"*
*loud as shit*

*Throwing money in the air, fuck it I don't care*

*50 for the earrings, that's 100 for a pair*

*Versace on my ass two bands for my underwear*

*Foreign cars, foreign broads, baller of the year*

*Sparkles on my champagne independence day*

*I ain't really want your number, your friend look*

*better anyway*

Quinton looked up just in time to see Tierra walk through the door. She saw that he was dancing with another female and looked pissed off. She walked up to him and looked at the girl like she wanted to smack fire out of her.

*"Really Q? I mean damn. Can you go more than twenty minutes without hitting on somebody?"* she asked.

The girl looked at Tierra like she was insane. She turned to look at Quinton and shook her head.

*"Damn Q. You can't even dance with your cousin without somebody trippin."* She said laughing.

Quinton was looking embarrassed because this was supposed to be his graduation party and Tierra was acting jealous.

*"My bad Keisha. This is Tierra. Tierra this is my cousin Keisha."* He said looking to see if she had drawn any attention to them.

227

Tierra looked as if she wanted to disappear. Her mouth flew open. *"I'm sorry."* She said. *"I thought..."*

*"Yea I know."* Quinton said walking off shaking his head.

*"Baby wait!"* she said following after him.

Quinton turned to her and let her have it. *"Your ass as fucking lost it yo. I ain't got time for all this Romeo and Juliet bullshit. We're done."* He said as he walked off leaving her standing with her mouth open.

*

Bishop was in his room putting on his sweats getting ready to go meet with Deuce so they could hit the main trap house. He looked in the closet at his sit that he had hanging up to wear later that night to take his daughter to her dance. He called Deuce to make sure everything was still set up as planned.

*"Hello?"* Deuce answered.

*"Whats good man?"* Bishop asked.

*"Wassup bruh? You straight?"* he asked.

*"Yea man. About to head over there. Is everything going as planned?"* he said to Deuce.

*"Yea man. They been set up down the block all day watching who has been coming in and out of there. Read and Quinton haven't been there all day so, we should be able to get in and out pretty fast."* Deuce told him.

*"Aight then I'm on the way."* Bishop said. He turned off the light closing the door as he headed to his car. He called Tanya to let her know what was going on. He had spoken to her a few times since the night they had the meeting at Deuece's spot.

*"Hello?"* she answered after a few rings.

*"Hey. We are on the way."* He said.

*"Alright."* She responded. *"I'll see ya'll in a bit."* She said as she hung up.

Bishop got in his car and drove to meet Deuce by the hose. Deuce had a car sitting parked down the street from the trap house to keep surveillance on who all was coming and going out of the house. They had a few of the younger boys walking the strip so that they would look like they belonged in the area and not to bring suspicion. Bishop turned down his radio and thought to call Anna to see if she would talk to him. He blocked his number in hopes she would answer. The phone rang several times. He was about to hang up when he heard her voice.

*"I know that's you Bishop. Calling me from a blocked number is not going to make me want to take you back so what do you want?"* she asked.

*"Anna, I, I just wanted to let you know that I miss you. I know that I messed up. I know. And I vow that I'm gonna make it right to you. And no matter what happens to me, I love you okay?"* he said.

*"What the hell are you talking about Byron? What stupid thing have you done now?"* Anna asked.

Bishop sighed and told her their plans. *"Look, we are going to raid all of the trap houses and take their bricks. I know you think its stupid but trust me, this is a way to save him."* He said.

*"Whatever Byron. Go be stupid. I don't care."* Anna responded as she hung up.

Bishop tossed his phone in the passenger seat and drove the rest of the way in silence. He pulled up to the park that was done the street from the house. He sent Deuce a text letting him know he was at the park.

*Bishop: Im here. Send the boys.*

Deuce was down the street when he got the message.

*Deuce: Done.*

Deuce made a call and watched six of his young boys and two of his original Soldiers coming from different directions.

*

Quinton was upstairs in the trap house getting ready for Traniece's dance. He had promised his sister that he would take her since for whatever reason their father couldn't. Quinton decided to send his sister a message to let her know that he was on the way.

*Quinton: Hey big head. I'm waiting on a drop off and then I'm on the way.*

*Niecey: Ok well hurry up because I don't want to miss the whole party case of you. Lol.*

*Quinton: Shut up. I will be there in a few to pick you up.*

Quinton tossed his phone on the bed and walked over to the mirror to check himself out and make sure that he was looking good for his sisters big day. He was also trying to make sure that he looked good for Maxine too. She told him that she may drop by so he wanted to make sure he was looking GQ sharp if she did. His phone was buzzing on top of the table that sat in the center of the room. He walked towards the table and glanced out the window on the way. He saw what looked like two boys running through the bushes towards the house.

*"What the fuck?"* he said as he stopped to look closer. He looked to the right and saw two more coming from the other side.

*"Shit!"* he said as he ran towards the stairs.

*"Load up! Load up!"* he yelled to everyone that was downstairs. He jumped down the stairs and almost broke his legs to get to the stairs. The young Soldiers were on the couch when they heard Quinton but by then it was too late. Before they could get up to get to the door, the house was bombarded in every direction with Bishop's men. Quinton had his piece in his hand and started shooting.

Almost instantly there were screams and glass breaking everywhere. Quinton jumped behind the couch and began to open fire on the men that were taking over the house. A bullet flew past him and hit one of the new boys Black right in the head. Quinton ducked and crawled over to him.

*"Black!"* he screamed. He stood up and fired shots to the door taking one of the intruders down. The bullet hit the light making everything pitch black. Quinton hit the floor and crawled towards the escape route that he had for the house when a bullet hit him in the chest.

*

**Chapter Nine**

Bishop sat in his car waiting to hear word from Deuce that the bricks had been picked up. He had been in the car a little over twenty minutes and was quietly listening to the radio when he got a text from Deuce.

*Deuce: So far so good. By the way, Tanya just pulled up.*

*Bishop: Ok. Tell her to stay put.*

The minute that he hit the send button, he heard gunshots and saw people running. He grabbed his burner out the seat, jumped out of the car and ran towards the direction of the shots with Deuce hot on his heels. The two ran up to the house where bullets were flying everywhere. Bishop began firing shots and ran in blinded.

*"Bishop! Right!"* Deuce yelled.

Bishop turned to his right and shot at the boy aiming at him. Deuce shot two more that were running out of the kitchen. All that you could see in the pitch black was the flashes of gun fire. Bishop was doing a sweep of the house and anyone that wasn't someone that he knew, he was shooting. He was so angry that he was shooting off rounds taking out his frustration on the house and what it represented. He was heading towards the stairs when he tripped over a body. He fell and could see in the dark that it was his son lying on the ground.

*"No, no no!"* Bishop yelled. *"Quinton!"* he grabbed his son who was soaked in blood and held him. *"Deuce! Call an ambulance man!"* he yelled. He grabbed his son and dragged him towards the door. Deuce, along with the rest of the crew covered him. He drug him to the door and down the stairs when everything went black.

*

*Beep. Beep. Beep.* Quinton woke up slowly to the sound of the machines beeping. Everything was blurry as he tried to focus on where he was. *Where the hell am I?* He thought. All he saw was white walls and ceilings. The room smelled of bleach and disinfectant. He tried to lift himself up but everything on his body felt like bricks. *Yo what the fuck happened?* He thought to himself.

He tried to open his mouth when he heard someone else in the

room.

"*Quinton? Oh my God he's awake!*"Tierra rushed to his side.

"*Quinton can you hear me? Don't try to talk. Oh my God. Thank you*

*Jesus!*" she rambled off. She grabbed his hand and squeezed it. It

was then he saw he was wearing a hospital bracelet with his name

on it, Quinton White. He tried again to open his mouth but

nothing came out.

"*Don't try to talk. I'm gonna go get the doctor.*" she released

his hand and ran out to get a doctor.

Quinton lay there attempting to sit up. He couldn't

understand why he was so groggy. Before he could move any

further, a tall white male came into the room with a chart. Behind

him followed a black nurse with what appeared to be a need in her

hand.

"*Well hello Mr. White.*" The doctor greeted him as he walked

in. The nurse walked past and began to check his vitals while the doctor went over his chart.

*"You are a very lucky man Mr. White."* The doctor told him. *"Try not to speak. I know you have a thousand questions racing through your mind, but right now your jaw is wired shut until it can heal properly."* He informed him.

Quinton frowned at what he heard and became aware of the metal that he felt in his mouth. He was starting to really wake up and listen to the man in front of him. The nurse continued to check his vitals and changed his fluid bag. *Where the hell do I know her from?* He thought to himself. The more she moved around him, the more familiar she looked. She paid him no attention as she continued to do her job.

*"Mr. White, you've been here for about three weeks now. You were brought in with multiple shot wounds and lost a lot of blood. We were able to remove three of the bullets however; one is lodged into your shoulder blade, so we will try again to remove the bullet once we know you are more stable and that your body will be able to stand it. But, for right now, you're out of immediate danger. It's going*

*to be difficult for you. I won't lie to you. You are very lucky to be alive."* He told Quinton.

Quinton continued to stare at him as the doctor rambled.

*"It's actually amazing."* The doctor continued. *"We had one gentleman die from a single bullet and here you are with four expected to make a full recovery."* He said.

Quinton frowned and rolled his eyes up. The nurse came forward with the needle and inserted the medicine in his tube.

*"What's that you're are giving him?"* Tierra asked. She had been exceptionally quiet throughout the time the doctor had been in the room.

*"It's just a sedative to help Mr. White relax and sleep."* The nurse answered quietly as she finished the medicine.

Quinton started to frown up again. *I just fucking woke up.,* he thought to himself.

*"I don't understand. He just woke up. Why is he being put back to sleep so fast? Shouldn't you be trying to figure out who did*

238

*this to him?"* Tierra asked holding back tears.

The doctor reached over the cabinet and retrieved some tissues for the girl. *"I understand your questions."* He said as he handed her the tissues to wipe her face. *"But that is a matter for the police to handle, not a doctor. Our job is to save his life, not try to figure out who almost stole it."* He said.

The young girl began to cry again at the thought of Quinton being gone.

The doctor came over and held her hand as they watched Quinton drift to sleep.

*"It's going to be ok. He's been through a lot. Better that he rest now. Because he has a hell of a battle ahead."*

*"And what about his father?"* she asked.

The doctor looked at her and shook his head.

*What happened to Pops?* Quinton thought as he felt himself losing consciousness.

Thank You's

Wow! I can't believe that I am on my second book! I want to thank you all so much for your support. First and foremost I thank God for the gift of writing. I was scared to pursue my dream and actually put my words on paper but, I thank you God for the strength to do so.

To my husband Michael, I thank you and love you so much! Babe you have really pushed me when I wanted to quit and I am proud of the MAN that you are! I'm ready for the Big T baby!

Even though they are too little to read yet, I thank my children Isaiah, Marvin, and Alexander mommy loves you so much! Everything that I do is for you all! Mommy is going to make you proud!

To my family, my daddy, (I won't call your name because I know how you are.) I love you much and thank you for your tough love. I know I am a handful but thank you for ALWAYS being in my corner no matter what. My mom, Morgan, we had a rough start but I love you for sticking it out with me and of course for marrying my stubborn daddy! Lol. To my siblings, I love you and wish you all nothing but success.

To my friends, of course first my bestie, Jesse! What up mane! Love you much! Thank you for being there for me and know that no matter what, we are always going to be besties! True friendship to the end! Janell and Doug, hurry up and get married! Lol. Nah but for real, love ya'll. You remind me so much of me and Mike it's scary.

To my FFCS fam, thanks for letting me hustle my books at the comedy shows! Lol. Ya'll don't know how much that means to me man! Proud of all of ya'll!

To my BLUtiful sorors of Zeta Phi Beta Sorority, Incorporated, ESPECIALLY to the DECks of ChaoZ Spring 2005 (Wani, Shamona, Dawn, Stephanie, Mecca, Shannon, Daphne, Monica, and Stacy), Thank you, Thank you, THANK YOU. I know I made the right choice. Z-Phi!

To my Sweetheart Sisters, Ow Sweet! Shout out to Gamma Lambda Omega Alumni Chapter!

And last but definitely not least, to the followers and fans of First Lady K, thank you so much for your support, your love, and your words. There's so much more to come so stay tuned!

Made in the USA
Middletown, DE
03 February 2017